The Stolen Ones

D0581134

C334328340

The Stolen Ones

VANESSA CURTIS

USBORNE

For my husband TB and in memory of my
great-grandfather Lewis Lubinski,
who was born in Chodecz, Poland.

First published in the UK in 2019 by Usborne Publishing Ltd., Usborne House,
83-85 Saffron Hill, London EC1N 8RT, England. www.usborne.com

Text copyright © Vanessa Curtis, 2019

The right of Vanessa Curtis to be identified as the author of this work has been asserted
by her in accordance with the Copyright, Designs and Patents Act, 1988.

Cover photograph of girl © Ollyy/Shutterstock
Cover photograph of girl © Ranta Images/Thinkstock

Extract from Love Song by Rainer Maria Rilke, translated by Jessie Lemont.

The name Usborne and the devices ♀ ⊕ are Trade Marks of
Usborne Publishing Ltd.

All rights reserved. No part of this publication may be reproduced, stored in a retrieval
system or transmitted in any form or by any means, electronic, mechanical,
photocopying, recording or otherwise without the prior permission of the publisher.

This is a work of fiction. The characters, incidents, and dialogues are products of the
author's imagination and are not to be construed as real. Any resemblance to actual
events or persons, living or dead, is entirely coincidental.

A CIP catalogue record for this book is available from the British Library.

ISBN 9781474915038   03984/1 JFMAMJJASO D/18

Printed in the UK.

Prologue

HE MEETS ME ON THE corner of the close, a little out of breath.

"Here, Inge," he says, kissing me on the cheek and handing me a small parcel wrapped in brown paper and tied up with a pink ribbon. "Happy sixteenth birthday."

It is not my birthday until tomorrow, but this is not a new tradition. I have been meeting Wilf the day before my birthday for three years now.

"Thank you," I say, stretching up to plant a kiss on his cheek.

"Open it," says Wilf, a shy smile on his thin face, his features delicate beneath his thick wavy hair.

I pull at the pink ribbon and the brown paper unfurls its stiff limbs, revealing a small red leather-bound volume.

"Rilke," I say, smiling up at him. We are both mad for the poet, but I've always borrowed volumes from the school library. "Thank you, kind Wilf." I know that this will have cost him money he does not have.

I open the page and read some lines at random, smiling up at him.

When my soul touches yours a great chord sings!
How shall I tune it then to other things?
O! That some spot in darkness could be found
That does not vibrate whene'er your depth sound.
But everything that touches you and me
Welds us as played strings sound one melody.

Wilf puts his hand on my head for a moment and looks down at me with his blue-grey eyes, the corners crinkling when he smiles. "Sixteen is special," he says. "It calls for a special present."

I smile back up at him, but inside, my heart contracts with pain.

"I wish you could come to the house," I say. "It seems so unfair that I can't invite you over after all this time."

Wilf pulls me into an embrace. His hugs tend to stop the outside world when I'm inside them.

"I know," he says. "But what matters is what we have

between us right here, Inge. That's what counts."

I nod, my face muffled by his shoulder, but inside I'm still hurting.

I want to take Wilf home. I want to invite him over to our house on my birthday and have him sit at the table in Mama's conservatory while she cuts into her home-made raspberry torte. I want my parents to smile at him and ask him about his life and for there to be an easy atmosphere of warmth and love all around us.

I hate that my boyfriend must remain a secret. I want to shout our relationship from the rooftops of Munich and discuss it with Mama over hot chocolate when we're out shopping.

But I can't.

I can never do this.

I will never be able to do this.

Wilf has been my secret for three years now.

And that is the way it will have to stay.

Chapter One

Munich, 1956

THE LETTER ARRIVES ON THE twenty-eighth of May, four days before my sixteenth birthday.

It is lying on our doormat among some early cards in their garish envelopes of pink and green, but this one is a plain cream colour with an unfamiliar name and our address typed onto it in neat black letters. On the back of the envelope is a box containing the name and address of the Red Cross in Bad Arolsen. There is a stamp, so I hold the letter up to the light streaming through the glass of our porch and stare at it more closely. Strangely it is stuck over another which looks far less familiar. I just have time to make out the letter P and the image of a strange man in a wig, before a hand comes from behind me and whips the letter out of my fingers so fast that I am left with a paper cut.

"I'll take that, thank you," says Mama. "It's not for your eyes."

She looks out of sorts. Usually Mama is up two hours earlier than the rest of us and I never see the first post, because she sorts and opens it before we even come down for breakfast. But today she has overslept.

"Why?" I say. "It's my birthday soon. It's probably for me." I say this in the full knowledge that the name on the envelope wasn't mine.

"It's not your birthday for another four days, Inge," she says.

I watch from the hall as she goes into the study, throws the letter into the drawer at the top of her mahogany desk and turns the tiny gold key in the lock. Mama and Papa each have their own desks. She drops the key down the front of her dress.

"There," she says, patting her bosom. "Not for prying eyes."

There is no point trying to wrestle it off her. My mother is a substantial woman, built like the typical *hausfrau*. Even in her flat lace-up shoes she towers a good two centimetres over my father and he is not short. Her face is large and square and tends to look stern, but when she smiles the sternness breaks apart and her eyes fill up with mischief. I guess that's why my father fell for her.

Papa comes downstairs and kisses me on the cheek as he passes. I give him my broadest smile. Papa is my best friend. He knows me better than anyone, even Mama.

"I will be making you a birthday torte," Mama is saying. "It contains both coffee and chocolate. Only the best for my Inge." She's referring to the chronic shortage of anything good in the shops. It has been like this since the end of the war, almost as long as I can remember. "We'll have it on your birthday at midday."

That's typical of Mama. She runs everything to a schedule in this house.

We live near the centre of Munich in a building full of glass and light and neat angles. I suppose from the outside it looks a lot like a plain box, but inside it is sleek and modern and there's plenty of space for three people and a cat.

Mama doesn't like to be caged in, or so she's always telling us. She likes air and space. I've noticed that when she's in crowds of people on the tram going through central Munich, she sucks her breath in tight and focuses her gaze on some point outside the window, as if the people packed in around her are invisible, or maybe as if she is – I can never tell which.

Mama chose the house five years ago. Papa just went along with it, as he often does. Mama took one look at the sparse white walls and smooth wooden floorboards and her face broke into that smile.

Papa is just the opposite. He likes to be part of a crowd and is often to be found propping up the bar at The Jugged Hare in Munich's old quarter, regaling anybody who'll listen with stories about the war. Life in Munich has become more relaxed since the military occupation by America and England finally ended last year. Although there is still not much in the way of luxury food, Mama can buy her beloved strong coffee beans from her favourite shop in town. She is very fussy about coffee. It has to be expensive, hot, black and strong. Anything else sends her into a bad temper.

My mother once told me that before the war she had wanted to become a concert pianist. We have a Bechstein concert piano in our living room. But then everything changed and, like so many German housewives, she found herself doing war work and sending parcels out to our soldiers and allowing refugees to shelter in the house.

I don't remember any of this, of course. I wasn't even five years old when the war finished. I know that Papa fought as a soldier and had to retrain to be an accountant once it was over, but that's about all I know.

It is eleven years since the war ended. I reckon that most Germans now view Hitler's rule of our country as a disaster, because of the ruined buildings and unemployment levels which haunt the cities. But I still hear people expressing anti-Semitic views from time to time and my father even has a painting of Herr Hitler hanging above his writing desk, which sits opposite Mama's. It's a small portrait of the *Führer* with his arms crossed, unsmiling.

My mother never mentions the painting. She rarely disturbs my father in his study, but I notice that once a week she flicks a duster over the faded gilt which runs around the edge of that portrait. Sometimes I run my finger over the ornate lumps and bumps of the frame. But Papa frowns when he sees me touching it.

"Leave that alone, Inge," he says. "Show some respect."

"Why?" I say. "Why should I respect him?"

Papa removes his glasses and rubs at his eyes.

"I meant, show some respect for my belongings," he says. "Anyway. The war is over now. No need to talk about it at home."

It's this sort of thing that makes me feel as if there is a large barrier between me and my parents, even though I'm so close to Papa in other ways. From what I've learned at school, the war was filthy and bloody and harsh.

Although Papa still occasionally seems proud of his role in it, Mama's eyes are full of a sort of remote untouchable pain, which I guess confirms the fact that ordinary people suffered more than anybody else. The streets of Munich are still peppered with bullet holes and lined with the jagged ruins of bombed-out buildings. Many men of Papa's age, who otherwise would just resemble workers in grey suits, are given away by a telltale limp or a half-closed eyelid. But I am lucky. Despite the lingering signs of the war, my life, at least, is easy.

Our family routine ticks on.

Papa eats breakfast with me every morning and then kisses the top of my head before departing for his office.

Mama takes care of the house and seeks out bargains at the market to try and make the evening meals more interesting.

I go to my school and get a thrill in my stomach every time I lay eyes upon my sweet, gentle boyfriend, Wilf.

My life would be pretty much perfect if it wasn't for one thing.

I'm afraid to go to sleep at night.

Chapter Two

THE WOMAN COMES NEARLY EVERY NIGHT.

That is why I do not like going to sleep. I fight it as long as possible. Sometimes I'm still awake at two in the morning.

I haven't told Mama what happens in the dream, because I fear it would make it seem more real, but I've told her I have the same bad dream over and over. Mama says that this is not possible.

"You have a nice life, Inge," she says. "You are lucky. You are not touched by war. You have a brilliant future ahead of you. I refuse to believe that your dreams can always be bad."

But I catch her observing me as I drag myself into the bathroom and stare at my reflection in the mirror every morning. I am as fair as both my parents, but some mornings my eyes are tight little slits of exhaustion and there are permanent purple marks on the thin skin underneath them.

I go to school surrounded by a thick fog of tiredness. I prop my chin on my hand during class and have a hard time staying awake while the teacher drones on about graphs and charts and triangles. But I can't fall asleep in the day either.

She could get me there too. I'm sure of it.

This is how the dream goes. It never varies. It's always the same.

I am young. I can't quite see myself, but I skip and giggle so I'm guessing I'm about three or four years old.

I am in some strange country where there are tiny wooden houses with smoke pouring out of their chimneys. I see a stretch of hills rise up behind the houses and the solid, red tower of an ancient church at the foot of the street, and I can hear the shouts and rumbles of men working in the fields. There's a tiny white school building near where I'm standing and a line of children in dark clothes are gathered around a female teacher in the playground. The warmth from the sun caresses my cheeks and I am wearing a little dress with blue flowers on and a pair of scuffed brown leather lace-up shoes. I am playing just outside a house and I know that inside this house is a safe presence. I never see who it is, but I am bound by something that feels like soft, strong thread to whoever is in there and although I'm thin and always a little too hungry, I'm happy.

I have a stone and a piece of chalk in my pocket. I wander a little further down the village street and crouch down on my bony knees. I sketch out a series of squares on the rough brown track and pull off some of the moss and weeds. Then I stand and scatter my stone at the squares and follow this up with a series of hops, one leg bent up behind me, scowling in concentration.

When I get to the final square I trip over my laces and fall flat on my face.

Tears rise up in my eyes but I struggle to my feet. The sun appears to have disappeared and for a moment I can't work out why.

Something is blocking it from my face.

I pull myself up to a standing position.

My vision is filled by something dark brown. It looks solid, like the old tough trunk of an ancient tree. But why would there be a tree in the middle of the street?

I reach out with my hand and try to touch it. It is not

solid at all, but made of a rough brown cloth. I try to push this aside like a curtain, so that I can feel the sun return to my cold cheeks. But underneath the fabric is something hard and ungiving.

The brown thing begins to slide down, and I realize it is a person. The figure reaches up one hand and pushes a long hood away from its face, which is now on a level with mine.

Two cold blue eyes bore into my own.

A voice speaks in a clipped, harsh language I don't understand. There is a wheedling, insistent tone to it that I don't like.

I turn to look behind me. I could be back inside the nice, safe house in about two minutes if I ran.

I start to edge away. An arm shoots out from inside the brown fabric and grips my wrist. It is like being caught in a vice of bone.

There is a commotion behind the brown figure. I hear the rumble of wheels and a whinny from an impatient horse.

The figure stands up, still gripping me by the wrist. I am dragged across my hopscotch board, my feet trailing the white chalk lines into an indecipherable grey blur and dust dulling the toes of my shoes.

My left ankle twists with a painful twang.

I want to open my mouth and scream.

But nothing comes out.

I awake in my own soft white bed with the red-rose patterned coverlet and, as always, I am so relieved that for a moment I just lie still, breathing in the scent of grass from the garden outside and the rich warm smell of Mama's coffee as it bubbles on the hob downstairs.

I look at my wrists. The skin on them is almost translucent and the veins are pink-purple and raised up, as if they've been iced onto my skin.

I swing my legs out of bed and sit for a moment on the edge, considering Papa's garden through the window. Asters and hollyhocks bend their necks together in the breeze and tendrils of ivy wind their way around the clay pots in which the red azaleas and china-blue buddleia grow. There is nothing brown in Papa's garden, apart from the faded potting-shed alongside the brick wall at the bottom. When I was little, I used to help him plant all the tiny seeds in the warm, crumbling soil and then use my miniature watering can to help them grow.

I shudder. My school uniform is brown like the figure in my dream and there is nothing I can do about that. But it is a colour which I try to avoid most of the time.

I am even glad that my hair is the colour of clear honey and my eyes are grey and that my skin does not go dark brown in the summer like my mother's does.

I reach out for the knob of my portable wireless and blast that dream right out of my head.

Mama cuts the coffee-and-chocolate torte at midday on my sixteenth birthday, just as she said she would. I have come home for my lunch hour.

We are sitting in the glass conservatory at the back of the house, a room used only for special occasions. There are plates laid with napkins, and an oval platter of fat potted-meat sandwiches with their crusts removed takes pride of place in the middle.

I watch as the chocolate cream from the torte oozes out onto the white china plate and my stomach does a little leap of anticipation. Papa has already stuck his finger into some of the cream and is sucking it down with mischief dancing in his green eyes, while Mama complains and smacks his arm.

He leans back in his chair, watching my face. "Little Inge no longer," he says, his eyes misting over. "You are a young lady now. Sixteen is not so very far off being grown up. And yet you still have your whole life ahead of you."

Mama sweeps a line of crumbs off the table into her napkin and shakes it briskly into the bin behind her chair.

"She is still a schoolgirl, Josef," she says. "There is plenty of her childhood left. Who would be in a rush to grow up these days anyway?"

Papa catches my eye and we exchange tiny smiles. Mama is quite often in a bad mood. I reckon she doesn't sleep all that much better than me some nights. She has not put any make-up on and her skin looks tired and grey even though her shoulder-length fair hair is as perfectly curled and coiffed as usual.

"Indeed, Anneli," is all he says. For some reason it always shocks me when I hear Mama referred to by her Christian name. I've heard it for as long as I can remember, but it doesn't seem to suit her appearance. "Well, let us enjoy some of this beautiful cake and encourage time to stand still just for a little while."

The torte oozes its insides onto the plate in front of me and a rich smell of mocha and fresh sponge wafts up as I plunge my spoon inside.

I savour the taste of my birthday cake. I am sixteen. I am lucky. I have had treats all day and my parents are spoiling me with food that mostly nobody can afford to buy any more. There's only one thing which eats away at my insides along with the coffee sponge. I can't enjoy things properly without sharing them with Wilf. And there's no way he could be here today.

Chapter Three

MY BIRTHDAY COMES TO AN END all too soon.

On Friday morning I wait for the school bus at the top of the close. The bus weaves its way past the pretty Marienplatz area of town and out into the modern outskirts of Munich where I attend the gymnasium. My school has a very good reputation and Mama has said that I should stay there until I graduate and go to university.

Students are streaming through the gates of the school building. The sun is harsh and high even though it is only just June. I am wearing my hair in one long plait down my back and I'm excited because we are to hear the results of an essay competition which I entered. I'm really hoping that I win first prize. I study every night when I get home from school. Papa is very keen for me to get a good education. He went to university before he became a soldier and now he's trying hard to get a promotion in his accountancy firm.

I wave at Wilf. He's in the year above me so we don't see all that much of each other during school days, but I like to know he's there, separated from me only by a long corridor and several classrooms.

Our first lesson is English. I am trying to learn to speak it in case one day I visit England. Papa says that London is just as cultural as Munich and that I shouldn't be influenced by what happened during the war. I get the feeling that Frau Hertz, our English teacher, still bears a grudge against England for having occupied Munich until last year, because she practically spits every time she mentions the place.

The morning passes as it always does, in a blur of scraping chairs, chatter, reprimands from the teachers and the bustle and chaos of hundreds of bodies moving up and down stairs and corridors at great speed. After lunch I sit at the back of the school hall and I wait for the judging of the essay competition. I get a little thrill to hear my name read out as the overall winner – all the studying was worth it!

I push my way to the front of the hall and climb the short flight of wooden steps onto the stage. Frau Smit, our headmistress, waits behind her podium with a glass trophy in one hand and a white envelope in the other. There's a roar of applause from the hall as I receive my prizes.

"Good girl, Inge," she says, close to my ear so that I hear every word. "You are a credit to this school, your parents and to Germany. The perfect Aryan child. Herr Hitler would be proud."

I let the comment pass. Most teachers no longer mention the *Führer* or describe people in this way, but rumour has it that Frau Smit was a key member of the Hitler Youth when she was a teenager. It is true that she has a similar painting of him in her office to the one Papa has in his study, except Frau Smit has hung a garland of greenery around her painting, softening the steely effect of the *Führer*'s stare and making him look as if he's decorated for St Nicholas's day or on holiday in Hawaii. Frau Smit also wears a red pin with the black insignia of the Nazi flag on it. None of the other teachers do, but because she is headmistress nobody has dared suggest that it might be considered a bit inappropriate now.

I clutch my prizes and return to my seat, flushing a little with my success and grinning back at the faces smiling up at me from their rows of wooden chairs. One of them belongs to Wilf and he gives me a particularly warm grin, so that my insides loop about themselves and

I wish that it was the end of the school day, when Wilf and I can spend time together.

'Well done," says Gretchen from my class as I sit back down. "Did you get the Hitler speech?"

I laugh. "Yes, as always," I say. "She is living in the past. How stupid!"

I mean this – although if I'm honest, I don't actually know much about the past. People don't like to talk about it. My own past is just Mama and Papa, our life together written in indelible ink on everlasting parchment.

But then the parchment begins to crack.

It comes out of the darkness.

I have been at Wilf's apartment after school, which means that I have had to lie to Mama and say that I was doing homework with a friend. In fact I was having dinner with Wilf and his father. They don't have much money but Stefan has a way of cooking the cheapest of ingredients so that they somehow taste good. We eat on our laps around the fireplace. Today was a home-made meat pie made of scraps of rabbit and it was delicious, possibly because Stefan poured ale into the mixture at the last moment. Having dinner with them is one of my favourite things to do.

The only problem is that Wilf and Stefan eat far earlier than Mama and Papa. So I have to eat two suppers on the nights that I go and visit.

Half an hour after leaving Wilf's apartment, I am sitting around the table attempting to force down one of Mama's stews. I am trying to ignore the taste of heart and liver by focusing on the fragrant sauce made of herbs and stock. There is a mound of mashed potato to mop up the juices and some rich red beetroots roasted in Mama's new steel oven. Her oven is the talk of the close.

The blinds are all still raised. Mama rarely closes them as she likes as much light and space as possible. So the lamplight from the buildings opposite ours is streaming in and I can see the silhouettes of people moving about their houses as they settle in for the evening.

I am talking about school. My trophy and envelope sit in pride of place in the middle of the dining table. The envelope contains enough book vouchers to buy at least ten novels. I talk so fast that I forget to eat.

"Finish your food, Inge," says Mama. "You should never waste good food."

Mama always makes sure there is nothing left on her plate. And if there are any leftovers, she cooks or bakes them into another dish so as not to waste a single thing. Papa, too, eats like a man who may never see food again.

After years of food shortages, he appreciates every mouthful, using his fork like a digger, ploughing it into the mounds of potato and then shoving each mouthful almost to the back of his throat. It has always been the same, ever since I was hardly big enough to see him over the top of the table.

When he has finished, he runs his hands over my glass trophy.

"Clever girl, Inge," he says. "We have brought you up to do well. May I congratulate myself just a little too?"

I grin. It is cosy in here, with the tall white pillar candle burning in the middle of the table and the flame reflecting in the glass goblets of red wine which Mama has poured for herself and Papa. The scrape and clatter of our cutlery is comforting.

After we've finished eating, Papa flicks through the sports pages of the evening newspaper and Mama goes into the kitchen to wash the plates. I hear her humming "Lili Marlene" as she slides the wet plates onto the rack.

I hear the noise before anybody else does. It's a sort of rustling outside the dining-room window. Something is shifting and fumbling outside the front door.

"Papa," I say. "There's somebody on the porch."

Papa regards me over the top of his black reading glasses for a second. Then he sighs and collapses the paper back into its original folds like a fan, before heading into the hall.

I hear the click of the front door as he opens it. Then a shout of concern, which brings Mama straight out of the kitchen, a tea towel clutched in fright to her chest. My skin prickles with fear. I've never heard Papa make a noise like that before. And I can see that my fear is matched by the expression on Mama's face.

I hear an unfamiliar voice. It is low and guttural and I can't tell whether it comes from a man or a woman. The voice begins to rise and then I can hear that it is a woman. She is speaking in a language I don't understand but I can hear the unmistakable sound of anguished sobbing.

My father's voice, at first understanding, begins to lose its edge of warmth and become low and desperate in tone.

I can't hear Mama at all. She has not spoken.

I creep towards the hall and press my ear to the door. My legs are shaking with fear. "You need to leave," Papa is saying. "Do you understand what I am saying? I won't have Inge's life turned upside down." My ears prick up at the sound of my name. Now I'm interested. I need to see who is standing on our doorstep.

I slide through the doorway and stand at the back of the hall. I can't quite see who is on the front doorstep because Papa has got the door half-closed and I can only see the back of one of his green-trousered legs and his red tartan slipper.

Mama turns round right away. It's like she has a radar fitted in the back of her head.

"Inge, go upstairs," she says. "Now."

The way she says it, there is no room for argument.

But I cannot move. Something in me says that I have to stay down here and find out who is on our front doorstep.

Papa is attempting to shut the door on whoever is outside. He appears to be winning. But then I see it.

A small, narrow foot in a cracked black leather shoe. It slides past my father's leg and plants itself firmly in the middle of our doormat.

There's a tussle, but the foot stays in place.

Mama looks back at me, mute and afraid. Then she glances towards the front study, at the bureau with the locked drawer. A quick glance, but I catch it.

Her face has unravelled from its usual smooth completeness into a mass of jagged angles and lines which don't seem to fit together. "Inge," she says again, but this time her voice is broken. "You really should go upstairs."

But it is too late.

The black leather shoe has been followed by a body.

A small, thin woman in a grey headscarf and a

nondescript long black dress has slid into our hallway and is standing in front of me.

She holds out her hands towards me.

"Kasia," she says.

I shake my head, confused. "Inge," I say. "My name is Inge."

She speaks in a faltering voice and a language I don't understand. But then she says one word over and over, pointing at herself the whole time.

"*Matka.*"

Chapter Four

I GLANCE AT MY PARENTS, at a complete loss as to what to do or say next.

"What does she want?" I say, backing away towards the kitchen. "What is she saying to me?"

The woman is creeping ever nearer. I can see the tough skin on her cheeks. She looks like somebody who has spent a lot of time outside.

"It's okay, Inge," Papa says. He has placed himself between the woman and me and is holding a warning hand out towards her. "You don't need to worry, this is all just a terrible mistake."

"What is?" I say. For once, I'm not comforted by Papa's attempts to protect me. I'm looking at the woman's eyes. They are a light grey, quite at odds with her worn complexion. They fix onto my own and relay a stream of silent anguish which I can't understand.

Things begin shifting inside me. There are thoughts jostling to be heard in my head but I can't pin them down long enough to examine them. Images and tiny jolts of feeling begin to rise up and cloud what I'm seeing in front of me.

A tiny grey house on a village street.

A dress with blue flowers.

The smell of something cooking. Beets, potatoes, cabbage.

Thin arms holding me safe.

A voice crooning a lullaby into my ear.

Mama finds her legs and moves fast.

She hustles me into the kitchen and closes the door.

"Mama?" I say. "Who is that woman? Why did she reach out to me? Do we know her?"

Mama has lost all her colour. Her skin is as pale and waxy as the candle left burning unattended in the dining room and her eyes have a wild, desperate expression which I have never seen before.

"Don't you worry yourself about that madwoman, Inge," she says. Even her voice sounds unfamiliar. It is tight and strained and the harder she tries to make it sound normal, the more I can hear the tremble trying to break through. "She is nothing to do with us. Your father will get rid of her."

But Papa has not yet got rid of her. I hear him talk to the woman in an unfamiliar tongue.

"What language is that?" I say. "That's not German, but Papa seemed to understand what she was saying."

My mother sighs. She knows that once I get the bit between my teeth, I don't like to let a subject go until I've got answers.

"No idea," she says. "Not one that I recognize."

Matka.

I make a note to look that word up. First I'll have to work out what language it might be. Papa has a whole range of dictionaries, so I'm hoping I'll find the word in one of those.

"I still don't get why a woman like that would come here," I say, braver now that my legs have stopped shaking. "It's as if she knew me from somewhere. But that can't be possible. And why would she think my name is Kasia?"

Mama drops a spoon into the sink with a harsh clank. She has spooned sugar into a cup of coffee and is drinking it with her back to me so that I can't see her face.

"I have no idea," she says, gripping the edge of the kitchen counter and knocking back her coffee as if it were rum.

There's one more brief, low flurry of voices in the hallway. Then the click of the front door and Papa comes into the kitchen, wiping his head with his hand even though it is not as hot as it was.

"These beggar women," he says. "Honestly. They pick on a nice-looking house and then try to ruin your evening. I've given her some money. She won't trouble us again."

Mama hands him a cup of coffee. I see a look exchanged between them. It is sharp and full of warning. I also know that if I ask Papa anything now he's liable to explode. Papa rarely gets angry. But something in his face is preventing me from saying anything else. So I help with the washing-up and try to block the image of the woman's thin face from my mind, and all the time my thoughts are racing ahead to a time when I can do my own investigation.

"Let's forget about it," says Papa. "We will refer to it as an unfortunate incident. No – in fact, we will not refer to it at all. Tomorrow will be a better day."

But tomorrow is not better.

The woman comes back.

She doesn't wait until nightfall this time but comes in the middle of the day, when Papa is outside in his shed and Mama is kneading bread in the kitchen. It is Saturday, so I'm hanging around the kitchen table, bored and supposedly shelling peas, but in reality feeling restless and strange. I can't seem to engage fully with the day. I would so like to see Wilf, but Stefan has taken him away to Berlin for the weekend. I always feel light and peculiar when Wilf is away, like a part of me has gone with him. Usually at the weekend we would be going to the pictures or strolling out in one of Munich's beautiful parks, sitting under a tree with our sandwiches and talking about everything or nothing in particular. I just miss him.

Mama is restless and snappy. I think she's been expecting something to happen all morning because it seems to be taking her ages to mix the bread. For as long as I can remember I have watched my mother's pale hands disappearing into a mound of oatmeal-coloured dough every Saturday morning, until her gold wedding ring is coated with a thin grey crust and she takes it off with a sigh and cleans it on a tea towel.

This morning her hands are fumbling with the dough and there's an air of tension hanging over the kitchen. I want to ask questions, but something in Mama's closed-off expression stops me and I know full well that Papa has removed himself to the bottom of the garden to avoid me in case I ask anything awkward.

When the tap comes at the door, Mama is already halfway into the hallway.

"Get on with the bread, Inge," she calls. "I will deal with this. Carry on as normal."

Of course I do not obey these instructions. I move into the lounge and peer out of the front window. It's the thin woman again at the door. She looks so small and bent and out of place standing in our very modern close of glass-and-steel houses; like she should be carrying a basket across a field and not standing next to Papa's polished blue-and-silver city car. Her skin is dark, so different from the fair smoothness of the cheeks of most of the women around here. Her hair, what I can see of it poking out from underneath her headscarf, is coarse in texture, with none of the smooth toffee blandness of my own.

When Mama opens the door, the woman does exactly what she did before and puts her small foot in its cracked leather shoe in between the door and the frame. She also drops a letter through the gap. I watch it lying on the mat and I'm dying to pick up it, but I don't dare move.

"I would prefer it if you would not do that," says Mama in her iciest tone. Mama is pretty calm and polite most of the time, but when she wishes to make a point, she knows how to have somebody back down in minutes with just a flash of her eyes or a tightening of her mouth.

But this woman does not remove her foot.

I hear her plaintive voice rise and fall and I guess she's

36

still speaking in that foreign language, because I do not recognize a single word. Papa has come in, dragged up from the back garden by some sixth sense. He walks straight past me and into the hallway. There's the sound of another tussle and an anguished cry, like that of a trapped fox, comes from the woman. The sound of the door slamming makes me jump.

The woman turns and starts to walk away from our house, but then she sees me frozen to the spot by the window. Her face changes, as if it has been plugged into an electricity supply, and she presses it up against the window, causing me to jump back in fright.

"*Matka!*" she says, over and over, pointing at her own face. And then something else, with her hands held out towards me, which sounds to me just like a meaningless spew of harsh foreign sounds: "*Chodź ze mną!*"

"Get away from the window," says Mama, not waiting for me to obey but dragging me by the elbow into the kitchen at the back of the house, where her abandoned bread sits flat and heavy in the middle of the table. I hear the sound of Papa drawing the chain across the front door and the heavy "whew" of his sigh before he comes back into the kitchen, shaking his head.

"She doesn't know when to give up, does she?" is all he says. He picks up an apple from the red fruit bowl on the side and heads back out towards his shed again. Mama hauls the bread off the table, throws it back down with a thump and begins to knead it out into a long, stretched line, before gathering it up and doing the whole thing again.

I try to read Mama's expression but she is very good at closing me out when necessary. It's like I'm looking at a painted-on mask and everything real and moving is taking place somewhere deeper inside her head. I know there's some sort of tussle, some sort of process going on in there – I just can't see it.

I feel sick when I think of the woman's face pressed up against the window, so close that I could see dark flecks in her grey irises.

There is something in the way she looked at me which has unsettled me right through to my spine.

Chapter Five

WILF ARRIVES BACK FROM BERLIN on Sunday morning.

It is like the sun has come out again. I always miss him so much.

We meet up in the old town and sit at a cafe which serves good chocolate torte, at a cost. I treat Wilf with some of my birthday money, because I know that he and Stefan have to watch every penny.

I had to make up another lie to tell my parents about where I was going this morning. It is hard carrying around such an enormous secret all the time, but I have to. If I did not, Wilf and I would have no relationship. It kills me that I can't take Wilf home, but this is just the way it has to be.

For my boyfriend, my beautiful boyfriend with the fair hair and the blue eyes is not just a boy I go to school with.

He also happens to be a Jew.

I'm pretty sure this is just about the biggest problem I could have as far as my parents are concerned. They don't speak much about Jews, but when the subject comes up the air fills with a tight, tense feeling and they avoid looking at one another or me, so I know that it's a subject best left untouched. It means that for the past three years I've had an inward struggle every time I have to lie to my parents and sneak off to see Wilf. It means that a whole big important part of my life is not shared with my parents. It means that when I might have wanted a mother to confide in about my boyfriend, I've instead had to talk to friends at school, and although most of them are not prejudiced in the way my parents are, they've got other things on their minds.

Sometimes I want to shake my parents by the shoulders and tell them that Jews are just people. Kind people, like Wilf. But although most kids my age aren't bothered by who's Jewish and who isn't, adults who lived through the war still have strong opinions on the Jewish race and it's obvious from my parents' closed-off expressions that they wouldn't want me to be spending my time hanging around with Wilf.

So I carry on living with my secret for every minute of every hour of every day.

I can't see how it will ever be any different.

Chapter Six

WILF TOLD ME ABOUT HIS mother just after we started attending an after-school art club together. Wilf is brilliant at art. I only went because Papa thought it would be good for me to do something creative as a contrast to all the academic classes that I take in maths and science.

From the very first day I noticed Wilf and his particular talent. The rest of us worked on still-life paintings of bowls of fruit and objects displayed on the window sills of the art room, but Wilf painted from his imagination and from the stories he'd been told by his father. At first, the art mistress was put out by his refusal to draw from life, but when she looked at the canvas in front of him and saw what he was painting, she withdrew back into the middle of the class and gave her attention to the other students instead.

Wilf's paintings almost always showed different sides of the same thing. There was a perimeter fence, and dogs with their paws up on the wire. Behind them, men in grey-green uniforms patrolled with dark guns slung over their shoulders. In the centre of the paintings were huddles of people in other sorts of uniforms – striped, or just made of what looked like plain brown sacking. They stood in groups, or sometimes Wilf had them digging or carrying objects towards different parts of the camp. His paintings were muted in colour – grey, black, dull brown, but sometimes there was a splash of red. Sometimes he took a detail from one of his crowded paintings and made it into a separate work of art. A woman having her head shaved by a soldier. A line of children with their heads hanging low being led off somewhere outside the main camp area. A woman with a baby in her arms hidden beneath a shawl, a look of fear on her face.

That one was the thing that Wilf painted most of all.

I knew that he was painting something from his life, but I did not ask any questions for the first few months of art club.

Then, after I had stayed behind once and we had chatted about art and books and music a little, Wilf invited me to come and take tea with his father.

And that is when he brought the story behind the paintings to life in a way that I was never able to forget.

"My mother was a prisoner in a place called Dachau," he said.

I was sitting in the faded black armchair by the fireplace that I would come to know as "my chair" later down the line – but on this occasion I was new, and a guest, and perched rather stiffly on the edge of the chair, trying not to notice how very little Wilf and his father had in the way of furnishings.

I was silent for a moment. We all knew what Dachau was. It was still there, inhabited by 5,000 refugees from Czechoslovakia, and Papa said that there had already been a memorial erected to the thousands of prisoners who had died or been murdered there during the war.

"Are you Jewish?" I said. Wilf had a fair complexion and light skin and the thought had never occurred to me before, but I knew that he wouldn't mind me asking.

"Yes," he said. "My mother was Jewish. But Papa isn't."

I glanced at Stefan. He was sitting with his head bent and his hands clasped across his knees. In that one position I saw angst and sorrow and a sense of defeatism.

"Papa could have been penalized for marrying a Jew, or even sent to the camps," said Wilf. "So he hid us with his friends for over three years. But we were betrayed by one of our neighbours, and although my parents managed to hide me with another of their friends, both Mama and Papa were sent to Dachau."

We were silent for a moment. I kept quiet and let the air settle around us.

Stefan lifted his head. His eyes looked weary. "The camp was liberated by the Allies at the end of the war," he said. "But a week beforehand, all the women and children had been sent by cattle truck to Riga in Latvia. And there, my wife was…"

He broke off and put his head back into his hands.

There was another silence. I glanced at Wilf, agonized. I didn't know what to say, or do. In the end I did the only thing I could, which was to mutter "I'm sorry" in the general direction of both of them.

"When I left the camp," said Stefan, "I found out that my wife was dead. So her sister moved in and helped me bring up Wilf."

"And then we made a new life here," said Wilf. "I help Papa with his locksmith business. People always need locks, so we do not starve. Quite. Although many people clearly are uncomfortable with a Jew fixing their locks.

But they recognize that they will get it done with more skill if we do it."

I put down the piece of cake I was eating.

Stefan laughed. "We're not that desperate," he said. "Go ahead. Wilf baked it especially for your visit."

Wilf flushed deep crimson when his father said this. It was the first time I'd ever seen him lose his composure. And from that moment onwards, I adored him.

We spent the rest of the afternoon playing card games in front of the fire and drinking endless cups of coffee.

From that day, we were bonded for ever.

Because of what happened to Wilf, I hate Hitler even more now than I already did, although I was only a small baby when he was in power. Knowing Wilf has just confirmed what I've known all along – that Hitler was pure evil.

I know that my parents were supporters of Hitler.

I try to ignore this fact.

It is not easy to do so.

Chapter Seven

FOR THREE DAYS AFTER THE strange woman's second visit, there is an uneasy silence in our household.

Papa comes back from work and has a number of whispered conversations with Mama. I strain as hard as I can to hear, but I can only make out the odd word and nothing makes sense.

During the evenings, the three of us sit around the dining table with the curtains drawn, and although Papa is deep inside his newspaper or doing his accountancy books and Mama is reading or sewing or helping me with my mathematics equations, from time to time one of them will shoot a glance towards the front path outside. Papa makes an attempt to keep things normal by asking me about whether I'm enjoying my classes at school or talking about things that we might do together at the weekend, but there's a strange feeling in the room which won't go away.

But the woman doesn't come back, and something in the closed-off expression on Mama's face and the way in which Papa exaggerates our normal family life by humming just a little too loudly or stretching his arms above his head with a yawn that sounds theatrical rather than genuine, stops me from questioning them further.

I tell Wilf though. I tell him everything. I need to be open with him, because I can't be open about everything at home.

On the Monday of the following week, the bell rings for first break and I drag him to one side of the school tennis courts and wait until he begins to eat his apple.

"Some strange woman has been coming to the house," I say. "And she seems to be looking for me. Mama and Papa are trying to keep her away."

"Oh?" says Wilf. "Where has she come from?"

"I don't know," I say. "But she speaks in a foreign language and has dark skin. She looks as if she spends a lot of time outside."

Wilf ponders this for a moment. I know from

experience that Wilf never rushes into saying or doing anything. That's one of the things I like most about him. He swallows the last of the fruit, his eyes never leaving my face, and tosses the core over his shoulder into the bin behind us – or at least, he tries to. It just misses and falls to the ground.

"Typical Jew," says a voice next to me. "Pick that up. We don't want your dirty habits in our school."

I roll my eyes. We get this on average about once a day and have learned to put up with it, but I'll never take anybody criticizing Wilf without giving something back.

"You're years out of date. The war's over, Marta," I say. "Time to move on now."

Marta Schmidt glares at me. She's the archetypal good German schoolgirl, with her blonde plaits and large, red-rimmed glasses. Her father is something high up and her mother is a typical rich *hausfrau*.

"Of all the boys you could have picked, Inge Krause," she says, pushing her glasses up her nose and sniffing, "you had to pick the only Jew-boy in the school."

I smile. I know that this will madden her. "I picked the best boy, Marta," I say. "I haven't any regrets at all."

Marta glowers at me. "You must have something loose in your head if you're going out with *him*." She tips her head towards Wilf without actually looking at him.

He's talking to a friend and seems not to be listening, but I think that he is.

I sigh. "So boring," I say. "Put another record on, Marta. And maybe learn to appreciate people for being human beings instead of labelling them according to race or religion, yes?"

Marta looks as if she is about to say something else, but the school bell cuts through our argument and hundreds of students spill out towards the various classrooms scattered across the site.

"The woman," I say to Wilf as we follow them. "What do you think?"

I notice that his cheeks have taken on a deeper colour since the run-in with Marta. Although Wilf claims not to be bothered by the stupid anti-Semitic attitude a few people refuse to shed, I know full well that it hurts him. Every time some idiot makes a senseless comment, he remembers the dark-eyed mother he lost.

It is still difficult for those who don't fit into that ideal mould of a perfect blonde-haired blue-eyed German child. I guess I am lucky in that I have Mama's fair looks and athletic build. Nobody picks on me, except for my association with Wilf, and I can handle that.

"I wouldn't worry," he's saying. "She's probably just some misplaced person living rough in Munich. There are loads of them still around. A lot of them come from Poland."

I picture the woman's face and clothing as clearly as I can after only two brief sightings of her. Although her clothes were not fashionable like Mama's or even particularly new, they did not look like the clothes of somebody living on the streets.

"Hmm," I say. "It's a mystery. And I'll get to the bottom of it."

Wilf smiles at that. He knows my character very well.

When I want to find something out, I usually do.

It starts up again on Thursday.

The remains of my birthday cake have long since been eaten and the silver paper plate on which it sat has been thrown away.

Mama has cooked a stew with a handful of dubious grey sausages she managed to get from the local butcher at the crack of dawn. There is still very little decent meat to be had anywhere. Mama says that food now is worse than when it was officially rationed during the war. She disguises the substandard sausages with carrots and potatoes and thick gravy made with onions, but it's still possible to taste the greyness of the meat, so we fill up on bread and try not to chew for any longer than necessary.

The three of us are sitting at the oak table in the dining room and I am pushing my food around my plate as I always do and then I hear it.

A gentle rustle in the hallway. The soft noise of something falling onto the mat.

Papa is off out of his chair and into the hallway so fast that he leaves a breeze behind him. Mama's face betrays no emotion but she puts her knife and fork down on the edge of her plate, most of her stew uneaten. This is very unusual. My mother serves herself small portions, but she never leaves food and she always encourages me to eat every scrap on my plate too.

Papa comes back in with his hands behind his back and an expression of disbelief on his face. He lifts the curtain and looks out at the close for a moment before letting the drapes fall again.

"What?" says Mama. "What is it?"

He sits down at the table and I see him slide something into the pocket of his trousers.

"Nothing," he says. "Don't worry, Anneli. Just that… situation that I thought I had sorted out at the solicitor's, that's all."

"What situation?" I say. "Why did you go to a solicitor, Papa?"

Mama is scraping the grey stew from our plates into one big heap of sludge. I feel my stomach turn over.

"There's obviously a loophole," he says to Mama. "I suppose paper technically doesn't count."

"It can go with the rest," says Mama.

My parents are speaking a language that I can't even begin to understand now. I've got a headache and my stomach is shooting up skeins of sour acid, although whether this is from the stew or the tension in the room, I'm not sure.

"Inge," Mama is saying, "go and get the sponge pudding from the kitchen, please. And there's a jug of custard in the fridge."

I sigh. Mama's home-made custard has limited appeal, given that there are not always enough eggs for sale and even sugar is still hard to come by sometimes. But I put the domed pudding on a plate and take the white jug of custard from where it is nestling next to another greying joint of meat intended for the next day's meal. Just as I am carrying it all into the dining room, I see Mama in the study across the hall, sliding shut the drawer of her desk and turning the tiny, ornate gold key in the lock.

She comes out when she sees me, snapping the light off behind her.

"Let's see if any of us survive the custard today," she says, with a small smile.

I'm not fooled. I know a diversion tactic when I see one. But I say nothing. I keep seeing that desk drawer in my head on replay, until it seems to have grown to twice its original size and be calling out to me for attention.

I eat the dry sponge with the lumpy strings of custard and I bide my time. I hatch a plan. It involves calling Wilf later that evening on the telephone.

When I'm sure my parents are busy, I call him. I speak on the upstairs phone as quietly as possible to avoid being overheard.

"I need your skills," I say. "Could you help me with something at my house?"

There's a silence. Wilf has never been to the house. I can tell that he is uncomfortable with the idea of entering the premises, in case Mama or Papa come home unexpectedly. But I also know that he will support me, so when I explain what I want to do, he sighs and says, "I'll be there. So long as you are sure that we won't be interrupted."

"I'm pretty sure," I say. "I'll keep a lookout."

Wilf whistles a little under his breath. But I know he'll be on my side.

And that is why I love him.

Chapter Eight

On Friday night I have the dream again.

It starts the same. It is always the same. I am on that wide street, the dark green hills stretching away on either side of the tiny village. I am jumping in my little leather shoes upon the hopscotch grid and I have left that house of safety behind me and am intent on my game, the sun warm on my face.

Then the shadow and the smell of that brown fabric and the grip on my wrist and that sense of struggle and panic and the blocking out of the sun by all that is bad and unknown.

That is the point where I usually wake up, with my own cries still sounding in my head and the harsh morning light streaming onto the white coverlet with its red roses like spilled blood.

But for the first time ever, the dream expands and offers me another scene.

"*Sie sind mit mir zu kommen*," says a voice, low and sinister in my ear. In the dream, this sounds like a foreign language, even though when I'm awake I know that it's German and I know what it means.

You are coming with me.

I begin to tremble. The smell of the brown fabric is musty, as if it has been in a dark closet for too many years. My wrist is hurting beneath the figure's cold white fingers.

I open my mouth and say, "*Matka.*" Then, louder "*Matka!*"

I look behind me all the while. But nobody comes.

"*Matka!*" I scream. "*Matka!*"

I wake with a gasp. The eyes of the woman who stood on our front doorstep a week ago bore straight through my half-asleep brain and cause me to sit up with a jolt. My face is wet with tears and I feel a sense of panic mixed with a determination so fierce that I get out of bed straight away and throw on my clothes.

The word I said in my dream.

"*Matka.*"

It is the same word that the woman said when she came to our front door.

* * *

I wait.

I wait until Mama has dressed up in her one good suit to go into the city and take coffee with her friends. She has been meeting the same women for years. They never come back to our house but always meet for coffee and cake at Cafe Heck in *Galeriestraße*. She returns home in a reflective mood after these Saturday sessions and sometimes argues with Papa about little things which don't really matter.

Papa goes to work at his office on Saturday mornings. I once dared to complain about this and was told in no uncertain terms that we were lucky Papa had a job at all, given the high levels of unemployment right across Munich.

"Who buys your clothes?" said Mama, her face rigid with disapproval. "Who pays for your food and the roof over your head? Don't you know how lucky you are to have these privileges? Why, some children never even got to..." And she stopped, her hand across her mouth, and left the room without looking at me.

Papa leaves first. I watch him drive his blue car out of the close and then I sit on the sofa with a book in my hand, pretending to be absorbed.

"You'll be alright, Inge," says Mama, as she always does. "I will only be a couple of hours. Don't forget to do your schoolwork and there's washing which needs hanging out."

"Yes, yes," I say, flicking a page of my book over as if it's the most fascinating thing in the world. In fact it's a school geography book and I've not taken a word of it in, but it was the first thing that came to hand. "I'll be fine. Have a nice time."

The front door clicks shut and I hear the firm tread of Mama's feet as she walks away to catch the tram into town. Other women on the close click around on high heels, their staccato tap thin and precise, but Mama almost never wears heels. She wears the same flat pair of tan lace-up brogues every day and only rarely gets out a pair of black heeled evening shoes for an event.

"I like to be able to walk in comfort," she said, when I questioned her choice of footwear. "Besides, it is wasteful to have more shoes than you need. I'm not interested in shoes."

It doesn't matter though, because despite her sensible choice in footwear and her smart but dull grey suits, Mama is striking enough to draw attention wherever she goes, although she tries her best not to.

I watch and wait for Wilf to arrive. He turns into the close about half an hour after Mama has left and he is carrying a small brown leather bag.

I let him in and show the way into our study. "This is where my parents work," I say. "This is the desk I told you about."

"I feel a bit bad doing this," he says. "Are you sure it's the only way?"

"Well, it's either this or I have to risk everybody seeing a locksmith pull up," I say. I stand by the door with my arms folded, until it occurs to me that I'm aping Hitler's body language from the picture behind me, so I let them dangle by my sides instead.

Wilf squats down and examines the lock on the desk drawer.

"Yeah, easy," he says. "But you'll have to explain to your mother why the drawer is open."

I swallow. I hadn't given much thought to how I was going to lock the drawer up again afterwards. Mama keeps the key in her pocket at all times.

"I'll worry about that later," I say. I go into the kitchen and steal some of Mama's special coffee to make for Wilf.

By the time I come back, the desk drawer is open.

"Oh," I say. "That was fast."

Wilf takes the coffee from me, gulps it down with a noise of approval and hands me back the cup. I see him looking around our house with an expression of bemusement on his face. It is the first time Wilf has ever been inside our luxury home. Compared to his cramped apartment, it seems ridiculously large for just three people to live in. I swallow my shame and give Wilf a kiss on the cheek.

"Good luck," he says. "I'd better go. Unless you want me to stay and look at the letters with you?"

I hesitate. Part of me feels like I need his support. Another part of me wants to be left alone with the letters.

"Do you want to stay?" I say, playing for time.

Wilf comes over to hug me. I feel the softness of his blue sweater beneath my cheek. "Yes," he says into my shoulder. "I want to share the important things in your life."

I feel as if I am moving in slow motion. I cross the room, loom over the open drawer and there it is. The letter Mama tried to slide in there without me seeing the other evening. But it's not the only letter. There are others underneath.

I put my hand in and lift out the pile.

The letters are all in the same cream-coloured envelopes and each envelope is stamped on the back with the logo and address of the Red Cross in Bad Arolsen. Our address is typed in black on the front, under a handwritten scrawl which is impossible to decipher. The only letter which doesn't match is the one on the very top. There is no logo and no typeface on this one, only a single word written in black pen on the front.

Kasia.

I open some of the other letters. They are all scrawled in the same handwriting and written in a language I don't recognize, on both sides of the paper and often running to several pages. The cream pages are dense with black, dotted with exclamation marks and underlinings which I can make no sense of.

They are all addressed to *Kasia* and signed *Matka*.

Matka.

"That's the word I said in my dream last time," I say to Wilf. I have told him about the dreams. "And it's the word that the woman who came to our door said. But who is Kasia?"

"That sounds like a Polish word. And why have your parents locked the letters away?" says Wilf. "It doesn't make sense."

I am silent for a moment.

"I have known this woman," I say. "Somehow. And she certainly knows me." But how? As Wilf said, none of this makes any sense. And it gives me a sick feeling in my stomach. "I'm scared, Wilf."

Wilf puts his arm around my shoulders and I lean into

him for a moment, inhaling the comforting smell of his clothing.

I know I will have to replace the letters. So I put them back in the exact same position, all apart from the very bottom one, which I keep to examine further.

Wilf kisses me. "Will you be okay?" he says. I look up into the eyes of my beautiful boyfriend and nod. I want to continue with the next part of my search. Wilf kisses me again on the cheek and leaves.

I go to Papa's bookshelf by the window.

I know I've seen it somewhere.

And there it is, the small blue volume which will help me unlock the mystery of these letters.

Mama comes back in her usual closed-off mood.

"I hope you put the washing out, Inge," she says, sliding off her black gloves and flipping them onto the hall table. She takes off her lace-up shoes and puts on her white fluffy slippers with a sigh of relief. "Is Papa back yet?"

"Don't think so," I say. "I've been doing schoolwork upstairs."

Mama gives me a look which I can't read and disappears into the kitchen to make tea. She is carrying a box of cakes from Cafe Heck which she arranges in a neat circle on a white plate.

"A treat," she says. "But touch the coconut slice and you're dead."

I smile. It's always a relief when Mama rediscovers her sense of humour. But I'm worried. If she finds that her desk drawer is unlocked, my life won't be worth living. I cast a nervous look towards the study door, as if that's going to make any difference. Deep down I pray that the thin woman will not return and push another letter onto our mat, for if she does, my deception will be discovered. The longer Mama goes without opening the drawer, the better chance I have of convincing her that she left it unlocked in error the last time she used it.

I swipe a coffee éclair off the plate. It looks expensive. I don't ask Mama where she gets her money from, even though she's a housewife so earns nothing, and they tell me that all Papa's salary goes into running the house and car.

"She probably inherited when her parents died," Wilf said once when I raised the subject with him at school. "Maybe they had a house to sell."

I nodded, but really I have no idea. I have never known my grandparents. Mama said that they died when I was very little, which means they must have been only middle-aged. There are no photographs of them in any of Mama's albums or anywhere else in the house. Papa's parents are still alive but they live in America so we don't see them very often.

"I'm going back up to finish my schoolwork," I say, my word muffled by the éclair clamped between my teeth.

"Inge, at least take a plate," says Mama, sinking down at the kitchen table and taking her coconut slice with a sigh. I grab a green china plate from the drying rack by the sink and scoot back upstairs.

Mama operates a strict no-key rule in this house. Other than her desk drawer that was, unbeknown to her, unlocked by Wilf earlier, we are not allowed to lock any door inside the house. Mama says it is in case of illness or fire, but I think it might be tied in with her hatred of enclosed spaces. Her own room is always full of air, even in winter, with the curtains open wide and both windows open too. Papa has to sleep in thick pyjamas all year round just so he doesn't freeze to death in the night.

I really wish that I had a key for my bedroom door, because I can't risk her walking in on me now. Instead I put a chair under the door handle, just in case anybody tries to come in. Outside I hear the high-pitched whine of Papa's brakes as he pulls into the drive, but I know he's unlikely to disturb me up here.

I sit cross-legged on my quilt and survey the thin cream-coloured envelope in my hands. I consider the typed Red Cross address on the back. *Bad Arolsen*. I look it up in my school atlas. Bad Arolsen is in Hesse, about 500 kilometres north of here. Then I flip the envelope over and look at our address typed on the front. With a hand that isn't quite steady, I open the envelope and pull out the letter from inside.

As I unfold the first page, a whiff of something distinctive causes me to start. It's a smell that seems familiar, only I'm not sure why. It's like herbs, or damp moss – a strange smell, but not an unpleasant one.

I open up Papa's Polish dictionary, get a pencil and pad from my desk drawer and begin my work.

At the end of the afternoon my eyes are beginning to film over from squinting and I've got a tight band of pain across the back of my neck and shoulders from bending over the letter so long. The pad in front of me is crowded with my pencilled scribbles. None of it at first glance makes any sense. The letter is scrawled in such a dense hand that I can't decipher many of the words in order to try and translate them.

I can read the date, however. It is several days before

my birthday and the year is 1948. So the letters began arriving here in this house when I was eight years old. And Mama has been hiding them ever since.

I think I am starting to work out the truth. I can hardly bear it, but my mind works it over for hours. And in the end, I can deny it no longer.

Somehow, "Kasia" is me. It must be. And Mama does not want me to know this, which leads me to think that she's frightened of something.

I know what *Matka* means – "mother". And I have seen the look in the Polish woman's eyes when she holds out her hands towards me.

I have to face the possibility that I am adopted. It makes me feel sick right down to my very core, but the more I think about it, the more it seems to make sense. I look at myself in the mirror for a very long time, seeking clues. And I start to see them. My face is a different shape to Mama's – oval, rather than round. My skin colouring is different to Papa's – it is still fair, but it has a slight olive tinge which never changes, even in the sun. And my eyes bear no resemblance to either of them. I have an oval-shaped face with grey eyes, just like the Polish woman. I'm amazed that I never really noticed this lack of resemblance to my parents before. I guess I just assumed things.

My mind buzzes. I want so badly to confront my

parents and just ask them, but that would mean admitting to having the lock picked and snooping, neither of which Mama is going to react kindly to at all.

So I guess I'll have to do my own detective work in private.

That evening I'm itching to try and piece together some of the few words I've translated in that letter, but supper time is dead on seven every night and nothing is allowed to detract from that ritual. So I leave it hidden with my notes in my pillowcase and sit at the table with my parents, as I have done every evening since I can remember. And while they eat the pork joint, which Mama has done her best to make edible, I observe them from under my lowered eyelids.

Mama looks pale, as she often does after her time at Cafe Heck. I know that she will be going to bed early with a painkiller. Papa is cutting his food up with relish and reading an article in a magazine at the same time, an expression of wry amusement on his face. He is wearing his usual leisure-time outfit of brown trousers, a white shirt and a green knitted sleeveless pullover on top.

"What is it, pumpkin?" he says. I jump. My thoughts have wandered off miles away. Papa is giving me his full attention now, his fork poised near his mouth and spooling an unappetizing skein of dark gravy onto the white plate. "You're very quiet tonight."

I smile and shrug.

"Don't shrug, Inge," says Mama on autopilot. She sighs and runs her hand through her thick fair hair. "I'm done in. Think I'll go up in a moment."

Papa doesn't respond. I have noticed that he never comments on Mama's outings to Cafe Heck. It's as if those afternoons don't really exist. And both my parents are acting now as if the strange Polish woman never came to our door at all, so it's like she doesn't really exist either.

Mama disappears off to bed, leaving Papa and I sitting in companionable silence with the rest of the cakes.

"These are delicious," says Papa, his eyes sparkling and his brown moustache twitching. "At least there's none of that damned custard."

I love it when it's just me and Papa. It's like it's me and him against the world. I know that he'll always be there for me, fighting my battles or giving me the strength to fight them on my own. Sometimes I try to imagine what he must have looked like in his soldier's uniform, but it's difficult now that he's older and has a bit of a stomach protruding over his waistband. Sometimes I want to ask how many people he killed during the war, or how Mama felt about that, but I know better than to ever bring up that subject, so I don't.

It's the one thing, other than Wilf, that Papa and I really can't talk about. I know I can confide in him about pretty much anything else. But there's that closed-off look on his face whenever it is mentioned in our house and Mama gets the same expression on too, so it's really not worth risking their bad tempers and then spending the rest of the day creeping about wishing that I hadn't said anything at all.

Sometimes I want to ask him to take the portrait of Hitler down from over his desk.

Every time I look at it, I feel sick because of what happened to Wilf.

All of this stuff flashes through my head when I'm alone with Papa. And I wish so much that I could ask him about the woman and the letters.

But as ever, this feels impossible.

I fork up the last dry crumbs of chocolate cake and wait for bedtime to come.

Chapter Nine

I GO TO BED AT my usual time, so as not to arouse suspicion, and I read for a while. Then I lie in the dark, feeling the rustle of the letter inside my pillowcase every time I turn my head. In my right hand I clutch the stolen copy of Papa's Polish dictionary. I am trying not to picture the face of the woman who came to our front door, but the harder I try to block the image, the more she seems to plead her way into the front of my conscience, so in the end I can't think of anything else.

An hour or so later, I hear Papa's steady tread and the click of the switch on the landing. I wait for the telltale creak of the bedsprings as Papa gets into bed and turns out the light, and then I give it another twenty minutes or so just to ensure that he hasn't forgotten to get a drink or brush his teeth.

Then I sit up and put my bedside lamp back on. I have a black pen and a notepad resting on my knees, as well as a magnifying glass taken from Papa's desk earlier. I am becoming quite an accomplished thief.

I slide the letter back out of its cream envelope and resume my laborious work, trying to make out one letter at a time, which is difficult, as some I don't even recognize. I just try to copy down what I can, and then I begin to flick through Papa's dictionary, searching for these strange words.

I work through the night and by the end I have assembled a collection of words and very few sentences, because a lot of what is written is indecipherable – at least to me. I squint through tired eyes at these words, trying to work out what binds them together.

There are some words which come up far more. I make a list of these against their translation:

Gospodarstwo	Farm
Nadzieja	Hope
Imie	Name
Kochac	Love
Zapominac	Forget

There's also what may be a place name, because it is written at the top of the letter along with something that looks like another line of address which is impossible to decipher. The place name is *Chodecz*. I make a mental note to look this up in the atlas.

By four in the morning I am wilting with exhaustion and my eyes hurt, so I slip the letter back under my pillow and fall asleep straight away.

I awake at six with the sun highlighting the red roses on my quilt and I pull the letter out and start again before Mama goes downstairs to make her strong coffee. Although I've only had two hours' sleep, my brain feels sharper now that the sun is pouring into my bedroom.

I work as fast as I can. Mama always knocks on my door at seven. I scribble down words, look them up, scratch them out if they don't make sense and then start again. At last I've got the correct spellings of the Polish words sorted out, so I can make progress with piecing together the translation. And finally I am able to make sense of the first full sentence.

One mogli zmienic wasze imie.

Be careful, they may have changed your name.

Chapter Ten

LATER ON, I LOOK AT these words and wish I had left them as they were, as a part of some other person's strange language in a far-off foreign place. I should have ensured that they stayed as far away as possible from me, Inge Krause, the girl who lives with her family in Munich.

Because once I understand what that sentence is telling me, I can't rewind or go backwards any longer.

I can no longer pretend that this has nothing to do with me.

I know that the letters are all addressed to me.

I know that "Kasia" is actually my real name.

And the woman who came to our front door?

I'm pretty sure that I was stolen from her, just like in my dream.

The woman who came to our door is my *Matka*.
My mother.

I need to be absolutely straight on my facts before I confront Mama and Papa. But after translating that letter, I know that I'm angry enough to have the guts to confront them soon. I need to.

I carry the weight of the words from the letter around with me for the rest of the morning. From the very moment I translate them, the walls and the furniture in our modern glass house begin to look different. I wander about from room to room, touching things I've known all my life. The oak dining table where we eat all our meals feels grainy beneath my fingers in a way I've never noticed before and there is a jagged crack down the central section. I walk into the kitchen and run my hand down the shiny exterior of the large modern white fridge, touch the cool silver handle that I open every single day, and I feel as if I'm trespassing in somebody else's house and illicitly exploring somebody else's belongings. I wander into the study and stare at Papa's desk, with the pen tray lined up neatly to one side, his spare spectacles and green fountain pen inside it. And opposite that, Mama's desk, with the drawer that Wilf unlocked and which I now cannot look at, because inside that drawer are the rest of the letters which have been sent to me.

Yes, to me.

There are the stacks of letters, all addressed to "Kasia" and warning Kasia that her name may have been changed.

And there is the woman herself. The way she holds out her arms to me and the look of pain in her eyes.

I can no longer hide from the truth.

Chapter Eleven

On Sunday afternoon I usually see Wilf.

This Sunday I feel as if I can't go over to his apartment. I want to see Wilf more than I have ever done, but I don't really know who I am any longer. He fell in love with Inge, the German girl who lived with her parents in a neat suburb of Munich. But apparently I am now a Polish girl by the name of Kasia with a mother I don't know, a mother whose language I can't even speak. A mother who is a stranger and who must at some point have been married to a man who is my real father.

I sink onto the edge of my bed, panic rising. If Mama and Papa are not my real parents, what am I even doing here in this house? These things around me can't be mine. My whole life no longer belongs to me.

I sit there for quite a while without moving. The thought of speaking to Mama and Papa about this makes me feel sick to my core. Mama will be angry that I opened her drawer. Both of them will be shocked that I have worked things out. There will be confessions, arguments, raised voices. And where will I end up after all that?

The Polish woman is a stranger. I've spent years running into the arms of another mother. I've got used to Mama's smells, her expressions, her moods and the phrases she uses just for me. I've eaten her meals and had my clothes chosen by her and been reprimanded by her and praised by her and it's her I run to when I am feeling ill or upset or in need of comfort.

I love her. She's Mama. My mama.

And then there's Papa. Ever since I was a little girl, people have commented on how close we are, how my eyes have the same twinkle in them and how we have been cut from the same cloth.

I've always been Papa's princess, his pumpkin, his only daughter and a source of pride.

I can't imagine a world without Papa in it.

Wilf's face flashes through my mind. At least he's still who he has always been. Suddenly I feel sure he won't let me down. He'll realize I'm still the same person he's always known.

I stand up, spurred into sudden movement by this thought. Suddenly I want to get to Wilf and his father as soon as possible.

I need something to be normal, the same as it has always been.

Just for the rest of the day.

I tell Mama and Papa that I'm going to see a school friend and I leave before they can ask me who it is. I didn't come down for breakfast that morning and pretended to have a headache so they would leave me alone. And now I know exactly where I'm going. I head into the old town at a run and stop outside the faded green door to Wilf's apartment block. I'm so familiar with the splintered paintwork on this door and I'm so used to the smell of boiled cabbage in the hallway that I don't even really notice them any longer.

I pound up the stairs, pushing past a woman who's trying to negotiate a heavy pram downwards. A small part of me realizes that I should have stopped to help, but getting to the safety of Wilf feels so important that I can't even look at her, let alone speak.

I arrive at the top floor with a stitch in my side and lean over the banisters for a moment, trying to catch my breath.

The door to Wilf's apartment clicks open. He's obviously recognized the sound of my footsteps.

"Inge?" he greets me.

Hearing him use my old name causes a knife of pain to twist through me. I have no idea how I'm going to tell him what I've found out. I've always been Inge, his Inge.

Then he sees my face.

He takes me by my elbow and guides me inside.

Wilf's father, Stefan, is in the tiny kitchen that leads off the main room of the apartment. He comes out to see who has arrived, wiping his hands on a tea towel and bringing a waft of some savoury dish out with him. My stomach rumbles, despite everything.

"Hello, Inge," he says. I get another shot of pain at the mention of my name, like I'm already mourning it. "Will you stay for some of my steak and ale pie? Light on the steak, I'm afraid. But the ale should make up for that."

I give a weak smile. "That would be nice," I say. "But I did not actually come for lunch. I need to talk to you both, only I don't know where to begin."

Stefan guides me to a seat by the fireplace. "Cheaper than coal," he says, seeing me look at the dried flowers standing in front of the empty grate.

Tears rise up in my eyes at the kindness in his familiar voice. For nearly three years I've been coming to Wilf's family home and Stefan is almost like a second father to me. As I think this, another shot of pain runs through me. For my own father – Papa – is no longer my first father. There is somebody else out there who owns that title.

"Goodness, Inge," says Stefan. "You are as pale as death. Whatever you need to speak to us about, it must be very serious."

"It is," I say, my voice cracking. I glance back at the fireplace, trying to pull myself together.

Wilf comes out of the kitchen and passes me a cup of coffee. The rich, earthy aroma takes me by surprise.

"Wow," I say. "Is this the proper stuff?" I take a sip and nearly choke. "How much of your sugar ration have you put in here?"

"Figured you might need it," says Wilf. He crouches down and takes my hands in his. I feel dizzy all of a sudden. I clutch the side of my chair and put my cup on the floor.

"Steady," says Wilf's father. "Put your head between your knees."

I do as he says. I feel cold and sick to my stomach and I can't seem to shop shivering.

"You're staying for lunch, no argument," says Stefan.

"You need to eat something. And in the meantime, you'd better tell us what's troubling you, Inge."

I raise my head and look straight into his eyes.

"I'm not Inge," I say. "You can't call me that any longer."

Stefan exchanges a glance with his son. I can see that for a moment they consider that I might be losing my sanity. But I have never felt so sane. It's like everything has been stripped away from me, leaving a stranger at the core, a stranger who is raw and open to the new world awaiting her outside.

"What do you mean, Inge?" says Wilf. "About your name. I don't understand."

I drink the remains of my coffee, grateful for the sugar.

"You can't call me by that name any more," I say again. "The letters in Mama's drawer... They are from that Polish woman who turned up on our doorstep. It seems I may have been adopted."

I say all of this in a dull tone of voice with no emotion attached to it at all. I need to keep my voice neutral or it will rise in hysteria and I might start to sob and never stop.

"No," says Stefan, crouching down in front of me and taking my hands in his. "This can't be true. Surely the woman could be a fake?"

I shake my head. "I don't think so," I say. "She's been appearing in my dreams for years. I believe now that they weren't nightmares but flashbacks. I'm sure I was dreaming of the village where I used to live."

Wilf sits down in the chair opposite me. He is shaking his head. "How could your parents hide this information from you for all those years?" he says. "What have they said about it?"

I sigh. "I haven't confronted them yet," I reply. "I'm not even sure what words would come out of my mouth."

Stefan goes back into the tiny kitchen and I hear the sound of cutlery being assembled and the gentle click of a spoon ladling something onto plates. The smell, even though I still feel sick, gives me a tiny pang of hunger.

"Eat this," he says, handing me a warm white bowl. I notice he refrains from calling me by name. "Then we will discuss it further."

We eat off our laps in companionable silence. I've had so many meals with Wilf and his father over the last few years that this, at least, feels normal, even though there is an unspoken undercurrent of something unknown and daunting beneath it all. Somehow Stefan has managed to make a meat pie taste delicious even with very little meat. I cut through the soft pastry and put a forkful in my mouth with a sigh of pleasure.

"Maybe some things don't need to change," I say, passing him the empty bowl.

Wilf takes my hand and squeezes it. Stefan gives me one of his warm smiles.

"You are still the same person to us," he says. "So let us discuss what you are going to do next."

Chapter Twelve

I ARRIVE HOME FEELING OLD and weary, but with a core of new strength inside me.

Wilf and Stefan have helped me hatch something of a plan. Wilf has suggested that I look through Mama's old photographs and see if I appear in any of them as a baby. It's such a good idea that I'm rather sore I didn't think of it myself.

"If you're not there," he says, "that's a major clue, isn't it?"

"You're brilliant," I say, kissing him on the nose. He flushes a little. Wilf is not good at taking compliments. He's the most modest person I know.

His suggestion means that I try and pace myself on the way home. I even pinch my cheeks to try to restore some of my usual colour so that I appear as normal as possible. Although a big part of me wants to run up to my parents and demand the truth, it makes sense to get as much information as I can before I confront them.

It is Sunday afternoon. I stand outside our house and look up at it for a moment.

I always used to be proud of our home. My parents were the envy of many, with Mama's paintings displayed artfully on the vast white walls of our living room and dining room. Other people's houses were crammed with ornaments and vases of plastic flowers and endless photographs of pets and children. Mama's shelves and tables were devoid of clutter. Her parquet floor was polished to perfection once a week by a lady who came in to "do", as Mama called it. Even Papa's desk, cluttered though it was with files and books and pens, had one of Mama's systems behind it. On closer inspection, the pens ran parallel to the pencils, the ink blotter was lined up to a neat margin at the edge of the desk and the oak of the desk gleamed with beeswax polish.

I look up at the windows of our house.

Another image flashes through my head.

It is the tiny house from my dreams. Nothing shines on this house. It is dulled by age and smoke and the chimney belches black soot into the air. There are no curtains in the two small front windows and there is washing draped out and hanging down from the sills. Mama would rather die than show her washing drying on the close.

Matka.

The woman's voice cuts into my thoughts. She holds out her thin arms to me again and fixes me with her grey-flecked eyes.

I shudder.

I turn my key in the door and go inside.

Mama is in the kitchen.

"You're home early," she says. "I thought you were going to be out all day with your friends."

I cast my mind back to Wilf and Stefan and I feel tears prick at the back of my eyes.

"Too hot," I say. "I needed some shade."

Mama turns around from the sink where she's rinsing a chicken under the cold tap.

"You do look a bit flustered," she says. "I couldn't get red meat. They only had these underwhelming chickens yesterday. I can barely get one meal out of it, let alone two. Anyway, supper will be at seven. I need to make a start on Papa's accounts while the chicken's cooking. Run and get me his ledgers, Inge."

I go into the study and select Papa's leather-bound ledgers from the neat stack on his desk. I'm about to leave when something makes me go over to Mama's desk and give that drawer a little tug, just to make sure.

The drawer is locked.

I hope that Mama still has no idea what I have done.

I stand by the door to the study, feeling sick.

Both Mama and Papa have concealed my true parentage for twelve years. They have lied to me. They have hidden letters from my own birth mother, because for some reason they never wanted her to find me. They must have been frightened of her somehow claiming me back and robbing them of their daughter. Or perhaps they thought that if I read the letters, I'd want to go and find her myself.

I have never been given the choice to explore my own history. Mama and Papa have just decided that they know what is right for me.

If that isn't a betrayal, then what is?

I steady myself on the door frame for a moment and try to compose my face into something neutral and unlikely to arouse suspicion.

If it wasn't for Wilf and his father, I would feel disconnected from everything and everyone in my life right now. I feel let down by my parents and afraid about what my future holds. When I walk around the house, even the floorboards under my feet feel as if they might give way at any moment. I feel different inside my veins, too. Like my blood has turned foreign.

I try to focus on the kind faces of Wilf and Stefan. I tell myself that they are my allies and will help me.

Then I head back into the kitchen.

"Here," I say, passing Mama the ledgers with what I hope is a steady hand.

I steal a look at her face while she's bent over the books at the kitchen table. She doesn't look as if she's hiding anything at all. Despite myself, I have a sneaking admiration for this. How is it possible to carry around such a life-changing secret for so many years without giving anything away?

Mama looks up.

"You're pale, Inge," she says. I flinch inside at the casual use of this name. "I hope that business with the madwoman hasn't upset you too much. I don't think she'll come again."

"She might," I say, in as light a tone as I can manage. "Who knows?"

Mama reaches out and pushes a stray piece of hair off my forehead. "I doubt it," is all she says.

There is a lot I want to say at this point. But I know it's not time to say it yet. I don't want to give anything away so I stretch and pretend to yawn. "I'll lay the table for later," I say.

"Good girl," says Mama, returning her gaze to the columns filled with Papa's tiny scrawl. "I could be a while here. Your father has many good qualities, but writing legibly is not one of them."

Your father.

Except he's not any longer, is he?

And I have no idea who is.

Later that evening I hear my parents muttering in the kitchen and the word "solicitor" is mentioned again.

I strain my ears but can't pick out anything else. So I spend the next fifteen minutes sitting on my bed, flicking through our family photo albums.

There are plenty of photos of me aged four and older. But none of me as a baby. I remember that I once asked Mama why this was and she said something about them being locked away safely as they were so precious to her. I have never seen any baby toys anywhere in this house either, or any tiny clothes.

I feel as if my feet are not connected to the ground any longer. How will I ever trust anybody to tell me the truth again after this?

My head hurts. I go into the bathroom and drop one of Mama's aspirin into a glass of water. While it floats and fizzes into a grey scum at the top of the glass, I stare at my own reflection – but it is as if the Polish woman's face is looking right back at me. I shudder and drink the bitter aspirin mix in one large gulp and head downstairs to try and have some sort of normal evening.

My papa has been at his club. He meets his pals there every Sunday afternoon and they drink too much beer and talk about the war. Mama always says she prefers him doing it at the club than at home, so she tries to ignore that he's in a far more genial mood than usual and keeps putting his arm around her waist and spouting nonsense.

I sit down at the table with my parents, as I have done every evening on a Sunday for as long as I can remember.

It is as if I am watching them from behind a veil. Or as if I am starring in a play. Nothing seems real any longer. Mama may as well be dishing out insects onto the plate and Papa may as well be reading a newspaper written in gibberish.

"Inge," Mama is saying, "you haven't eaten much. Don't you like it?"

I eat another piece of chicken under her watchful gaze. The turmoil inside my heart is affecting my stomach and I am finding it hard to get the food down.

"I ate too much with my friends," I say. "Sorry."

Papa is looking at me now over the top of his glasses. It is unusual for me not to finish my supper.

"Are you sickening for something, pumpkin?" he says. At this use of my nickname, the urge to cry becomes overwhelming.

"Maybe," I say. "I do have a bit of a headache."

Mama goes into the kitchen and comes back looking pleased with herself.

"I managed to get a treat," she says, opening a tub of ice cream. "It is only vanilla, but still."

Papa puts down his paper and rubs his hands.

I can see that Mama is being kind so I force down a mouthful of the ice cream and then push back my chair.

"I think I'll go to bed," I say. "I don't want to miss school tomorrow."

That, of course, is a lie as well. I don't care about school. But I do want to be feeling as strong as I can for what I've got to do in the morning.

"Alright, Inge?" says Mama. She looks concerned now. "Do you want me to bring you up a hot drink?"

I know she's trying to be caring but even so, it all seems like some sort of futile act now.

"No," I say. "I just want to be left alone."

I walk out of the kitchen so as not to see their faces.

Chapter Thirteen

I AM LYING IN BED underneath Mama's embroidered quilt and running my hands over the outlines of the stitched roses for comfort. I've been doing this since I was a little girl. It always made me feel safe and secure, but today the only thing which still feels safe and secure is my relationship with Wilf and his father.

I get up earlier than usual.

"I am going in to school to play tennis," I say, walking into the kitchen with my racket poking out of my school bag.

Papa looks pleased. "Good girl," he says. "It is so important to keep fit and healthy."

I feel a pang of guilt as I slam the front door behind me. It's so early on the close that most of the men haven't left for work yet and many curtains are still drawn.

I walk to school through the Altstadt to save waiting ages for a bus. I pass the glockenspiel with its colourful figures and the *Altes Rathaus*, our old town hall, with the pointed green and brown spires. I always shudder a little when I pass this building, as Stefan once told me that Joseph Goebbels made a speech here which culminated in the dreadful *Kristallnacht* of 1938, when Jewish shopkeepers had their windows smashed in, and synagogues and cemeteries were vandalized by the Nazis and many people were killed. Stefan said that 30,000 Jews had been sent to concentration camps as a result of that night.

Today I don't shudder, or even notice the building in the way I usually do. I am disconnecting myself from everything familiar, everything German. In my head I'm thinking about the tiny run-down house that I first saw in a dream even before the Polish woman turned up here, and I can't help comparing the dirt track outside that house and the cluster of tiny buildings huddled together with the grand gothic buildings of the city I've loved and grown up in.

By the time I get to school I feel quite exhausted from the intensity of my thoughts. I need to find Wilf.

I'm pretty sure he'll be up in the art room working on a painting that he's submitting for his exam soon.

I pound up the ornate staircase, ignoring a startled look from the caretaker.

Wilf has his back to the door as I enter the art studio and I can tell that he is concentrating hard on what he is doing. My heart lifts at the sight of him.

"You're early," says Wilf. "Did you manage to get a look at the family album?"

"Yes. There were no photos of me as a baby at all. Not a single one."

"Oh, Inge. I'm sorry," says Wilf.

"So I need your help," I say, straight to the point. Wilf glances one last time at his painting and puts his brush down. I notice that he's added in some tiny figures looking out of a window in what appears to be a barracks. There's a desolate feeling coming from the figures even though I can't really see their faces.

"Name it," he says. His face looks strained and a little gaunt. My kind, unselfish boyfriend. And now I'm adding to his worry with a whole heap of my own.

"I need to use your telephone," I say. "I can't use the one at home as Mama is there. And there's no way I can use the office one here. I need to ring up the Red Cross and ask about those letters."

Wilf doesn't ask questions. That's one of the many things I like about him. Whenever I ask for anything at home I have to justify my reasons. But Wilf just trusts me. And he knows I need to do this. He fishes around in the pocket of his worn brown corduroy jacket and pulls out two long keys on a battered leather keyring.

"Here," he says. "You know you'll be late for class, though."

I nod. "Some things are more important," I say. I turn to leave and then come back again and kiss his cheek. "I'll leave you to your painting," I say. I hold his gaze for a moment and torrents of emotion pass between us without us actually having to speak.

There's so much sadness living inside him, along with other things which are hard to process. I'm starting to understand how that feels.

"See you later, beautiful girl," he says, already returning to his painting.

"I don't feel very beautiful," I say. "Just confused."

Wilf turns round and gives me his gentle smile. "I don't care what you think," he says. "I will always think of you as beautiful."

I give a tired grin. Then I run back down the stairs.

It's the first time I've ever been inside Wilf's apartment without either him or his father being there too. It feels very different without the warmth of their personalities to detract from the shabbiness of the rooms. I wander about for a moment, trying to pluck up the courage to lift the telephone receiver and do what I have to do. I'm well aware that I'm hovering on the periphery between my old life and my new one and everything could change for good in a few minutes' time, so it seems important to extend the old life for just a few moments longer.

I drift around the living room, looking at the photographs on the walls and the old armchairs by the fire with their stuffing starting to poke through the black fabric. I stick my head into Wilf's bedroom and look at the neat bed, made to perfection, and the one shelf of books over the headboard. I go over to Wilf's desk and look down at the pens and notepads lined up from last night's homework and at the two pairs of worn brown leather lace-up shoes tucked under the bed. Then I wander into Stefan's bedroom and gaze around. I touch the shaving brush in its mug on a shelf above the sink and pick up a book from the bedside table. It's an old edition of short stories which gives off a whiff of history as I flick through the pages. A pair of spectacles sits in an open case next to it and there's a bottle of pills by the bedside lamp.

Everything is very neat and orderly, but there's something about the room which makes me feel lifeless and depressed. I struggle for a moment, trying to work out what it is. At first I assume it's just because I'm in the apartment without its occupants. But then I realize what it is.

Everything is very male.

No patterned carpets or curtains, no fragranced soaps, no scent of perfume in the air. Even in the kitchen, everything is neat and functional but there are no bottles of jam or fruit, no ironing board in evidence, even though I know that Stefan cooks and irons for himself and Wilf.

But it feels exactly like what it is – a bachelor flat for two males. I feel as if I shouldn't be here, even though Wilf said it was okay. And I'm nervous about making the phone call.

I go back into the living room and lift the heavy black receiver off its cradle. Even the telephone feels unused, which it mainly is. Phone calls cost money and Wilf's father doesn't have any. I've already planned to leave them some money to cover this call.

I take one more look around the flat. Then I steel myself. It's just a phone call, after all. If I approach it in a businesslike way then perhaps it will feel less momentous.

After two rings, a woman's voice answers.

Chapter Fourteen

"MY NAME IS – WAS – INGE KRAUSE," I say. "I've been receiving letters with the Red Cross address on them and I think they're from my birth mother. I want to find out why my parents have been hiding them from me. I also want to find out more about where I come from and who my parents are."

An image of Papa comes to my mind when I say this. I swallow. I've always been so close to Papa. He's never acted in any way other than as a loving and supportive father. For the first time I feel a stab of guilt. What am I about to do to him and Mama? Although my own world has been shattered, maybe I'm about to shatter theirs as well. This has never occurred to me until now.

"Are you still there?" says the receptionist. "I'm putting

you through to our international tracing department. Hold the line."

I fiddle with the frayed edges of Stefan's favourite armchair while I'm waiting. I'm perched on the arm of it, banging my leg against the side and trying to pretend that this is no big deal, any of it. From time to time I glance outside. Even though Stefan is lovely, I don't much fancy him coming home and finding me in his apartment with no warning.

There's a click on the line and another voice answers, this time male.

I repeat the same thing I've just told the receptionist and there's a little pause.

"Okay," says the man. "So just to confirm, you want to find out more about your birth parents?"

"Yes," I say. "I found some letters with your address on. So I figured you'd be a good place to start."

"How old are you, please?" asks the man.

"Sixteen," I say, in what I hope is a very mature and responsible way.

"Okay," says the man again. I somehow know that what he's about to say will be anything but okay. "You need to speak to your adoptive parents first. I can't give out information over the telephone, given your age. I suggest you talk it through with them and perhaps then all three of you can visit our offices in Bad Arolsen and we'll see what we can do."

I get a nasty sick feeling at the term "adoptive parents". Even though I'm now sure that's what they are, I guess there's still a tiny part of me which is hoping that all of this is a dreadful mistake and we can all go back to normal as if nothing has happened.

"Is there no other way I can get information?" I say. "I haven't told my parents – my adoptive parents – that I've found the letters yet. They don't know that anything is wrong."

"Ah, I see," says the man. "Well, even more reason for you to sit down and discuss things with them first. Please do contact us again and we will try to help you then."

I hang up and sit on the edge of the chair for a while longer, gazing down at the people walking on the cobbled streets below without really seeing them. The thought comes into my head that I could ring back and lie about my age, but I suspect that if the same person answered the phone they'd know it was me again straight away.

I am going to have to talk to my parents. But the thought of doing it makes me shiver. I don't know what reaction I'm going to get, but one thing I do know is that it's not going to be an easy conversation. I realize now that, as well as changing my entire life, this discussion is going to change the lives of Mama and Papa as well.

I have classes to get to, which will delay the agony of what lies ahead for better or worse. I picture Wilf's gentle face and imagine his warm arms around my waist. Thank goodness I have support there – a lifeline.

I take a last look around the apartment. Now that I've been here a while I feel reluctant to leave it. There's something comforting about the faint scent of Stefan's shaving soap mingled with what smells like vegetable soup.

I lock up the apartment and go back to school to somehow try to get through the day.

It is gone half past five by the time I drag my feet up the front path of our house. I spent as much time dawdling at school after lessons as I could. I surprised the art teacher by offering to help her clear up after a messy afternoon of oil painting and then I shocked the school caretaker by asking if he wanted any help locking up.

"I can't allow a pupil to lock up the school," he said, in an affronted tone of voice. "That's more than my job's worth. You shouldn't be wandering about the place at this time anyway."

He ushered me towards the main school doors and watched until I'd gone down the steps outside and headed off in the direction of home.

Mama greets me looking pale and angry and relieved all at once.

"Inge, you're over an hour late," she says. "What on earth have you been doing? It's not gym club tonight, is it?"

"No," I say. A great weariness has just come over me. I want to go upstairs to my bedroom and hide under my quilt for a few days and emerge to find that this has all been a dream.

"Well?" says Mama, hand on hip in the hallway. She's got flour on her hands and is wearing her usual white apron with a splatter of red roses patterned over it. "Why are you late then?"

We're saved by Papa shuffling into the hall in his slippers, pipe sticking out of his mouth and a newspaper folded in one hand. He smiles when he sees me.

"Oh, there you are, pumpkin," he says. "We were about to send out a search party. Still, no harm done." He kisses the top of my head and disappears into his study to avoid having to hear what Mama says to me next. Papa is not a big fan of confrontation.

"Inge," says Mama, "my bread will have risen to the

ceiling by the time I get an answer from you. For the last time, where have you been?"

I push past her and go to get some juice out of the fridge. "I just decided to do my homework at school," I say. "No big deal."

Mama follows me into the kitchen and whips the juice bottle out of my hand, pours some into a glass and passes me that instead.

"Well, next time let me know," she says. "I was worried about you."

I nod, but I know deep down that there's not going to be a next time so I don't give it another thought. My head is churning with mixed-up sentences. I'm trying to rehearse what I need to say, only it's all muddled up and the determination I felt on the walk back from school is evaporating in direct relation to Mama's words and actions around the kitchen. It all feels so very normal and yet nothing's normal now. I feel exhausted with the effort of trying to appear as if I'm fine.

"I'm going to finish that homework in my room," I say. Then I duck out of the kitchen before Mama has a chance to say anything. She won't interfere with my schoolwork so I reckon I've got one hour before I'm called down to dinner.

One hour to get my head together. One hour to

practise the words which are not only going to change my life but might break my parents' hearts. I don't know. I have no way of knowing how they are going to react.

I sit cross-legged on my bed, watching the clock.

I sit frozen like that for an hour. I don't move, read, or even think that much. I just sit.

"Inge, supper," calls Mama from the foot of the steps.

It's time. I take a last look at my bedroom, then I go downstairs.

I walk into the dining room and it all looks different, like the set in a stage play with my parents in the leading roles. Papa is putting a pot of soup on the table and Mama is untying her apron and folding it into a neat square as she always does, before placing it on the back of her chair and sitting down with a sigh. I've seen this happen so often and never thought anything of it, but tonight every movement seems to have slowed down and taken on a greater significance. The lamps throw light onto the dining table but the rest of the room is starting to get dark, which only adds to the sensation that I'm sitting in a theatre seat and watching the spotlight fall on two people in front of me as they begin to play out the drama of my life.

I sit down and stir the soup with my spoon, releasing a great waft of steam which smells of barley and onion.

"I couldn't get any meat again," says Mama with an apologetic smile. "I'm running out of ways to make soup more interesting."

She stares into her own bowl for a moment as if she's thinking of something else, but then jolts back into action and offers round a plate of brown bread.

"I thought perhaps we might have an outing at the weekend," says Papa, tearing off chunks of bread and dropping them into his bowl, where they become saturated with soup and sink to the bottom. "Maybe go out to a park or take in a film. What do you fancy, pumpkin?"

I look up, startled. I've been rehearsing words in my head and trying to find the courage to speak them, but so far I just feel frozen to my chair and unable to think straight. And now Papa is suggesting an outing. He rarely does that. Usually he spends most of his time in the office, his club or the garden shed.

"I fancy a show," says Mama. "A musical or something with a bit of life in it. What do you think, Inge?"

I think that I am confused. They're showing me a lot of attention this evening and trying to jolly me along, almost as if they know I'm sinking into despair. But how can they? I've been very careful not to give anything away.

I've not said or done a single thing to arouse suspicion since the day I removed the letter from Mama's drawer.

"Yes, alright," I say. But I get a shot of something sour coming up from my stomach. I realize that it's adrenalin and that it's about to propel me forward, even if I don't want to go there any longer.

"No," I say. "Actually it's not alright. I need to talk to you both about something."

Papa glances at Mama and takes his reading glasses off. Mama lowers her spoon with great care and puts it at the side of her plate, lining it up straight as if she's playing for time.

"I read some letters," I say, surprising myself at how I get straight to the point. "From the drawer in Mama's desk."

I stop then, trying to gauge their reactions. Mama is frowning at me as if she's trying to see straight into my soul. Papa's hands are shaking a little.

"Letters?" he says. "What letters?"

Mama pushes her bowl away and gives him one of her looks.

"Oh, stop it, Josef," she says. "It's a bit late to pretend, isn't it? You'll just make yourself look ridiculous."

"Pretend what?" I say. Now it's me who has started to shake, as if I've been plugged into a low-voltage socket.

"We know you've found the letters," says Mama. "I

saw that the pile had been disturbed."

I nod. In a way I appreciate her just coming out and saying it. There doesn't seem much point dropping clues and playing guessing games at this stage.

"Why didn't you tell me you knew, or ask me anything?" I say. "Were you hoping you were wrong about me having found the letters?"

Papa looks lost. He is staring from Mama to me and back again, and his brown eyes are glistening with moisture.

"Yes, I suppose so," says Mama. "I was also hoping that you would not understand what was in them. But we saw that you had taken Papa's Polish dictionary too."

I flush. I thought I'd hidden my tracks very well but I had kept that dictionary up in my bedroom for two days. I'd thought nobody would notice the tiny gap in the bookshelves in Papa's study, but I forgot how observant Mama is. She doesn't miss a trick.

This isn't going quite as I imagined it would. I am thrown by the fact that my parents already know I took the letters and have translated them. This makes a big part of my revelation redundant. We have hurtled towards the heart of the matter almost right away.

"Well?" says Mama. "You have questions you want to ask us, Inge. So ask them."

I look at Papa. Mama's matter-of-fact tone is chilling me. I thought she would reach out right away and reassure me, but instead her face has closed off and looks cold.

"Go easy, Anneli," he says. "This is our child you are talking to."

"Or not," I say. "That's the problem really, isn't it? I'm not your child."

Papa reaches out and places his warm brown hand over my small white one. "You will always be our child," he says. "There is more to being a parent than just conceiving and giving birth, Inge."

"Kasia," I say on autopilot. "That's my name, isn't it?"

"It is not the name we chose for you," says Mama. "I called you Inge after my mother."

"The mother you never saw?" I say. "The grandmother I never met, who's now dead? And I suppose it doesn't matter anyway, as I'm not related to her."

I can feel the anger rising up in me at last. It's almost a relief after feeling so numb.

It is Mama's turn to flush. Her pale skin flames an angry red and her eyes, like Papa's, begin to fill with water.

"You know very little," she says. "So I will tell you what I can. Josef, put the kettle on. I'll have a sugar in my coffee, if you can find any."

For once, Papa doesn't make a joke or pull a face when

she says this. He leaves the room and I can hear him getting the cups out of the kitchen cupboards and murmuring to himself under his breath.

Mama waits until he has come back in with a tray. Those three minutes between us feel like the longest silence in history. I don't know where to look any more, and neither does Mama. We are becoming strangers. When she passes me my cup and I say "Thank you", it sounds as if I am addressing somebody I've never known.

"Yes, we adopted you," says Mama, after a large gulp of her coffee. "We were unable to have children of our own. So we applied to an adoption centre towards the end of the war and we got you."

"What sort of adoption centre?" I say. It seems important that I should know every detail of this part of my life that I never knew existed.

"That doesn't matter," says Mama. "What matters is that you needed a good home and we gave you one. We have brought you up well and you have had everything you could have wished for. So as far as I am concerned, you are still my daughter and I am still your mother."

Papa is looking at me. He knows me very well. He knows that I won't stop until I have the truth.

"But my real mother has been to this house," I say. There seems no point denying this any longer. "I know that it was her who wrote me those letters and that you hid them from me for years. Do you know her? Is that how she knew where we lived?"

Again, my parents swap glances. I wish they wouldn't. I'm not sure whether they're considering telling me some rehearsed story or floundering for something to say to appease me. Either way, I'm getting the feeling that there are gaps in this tale which are not going to be filled in tonight.

"We don't know her," says Papa. "In fact, we did not really know who your birth mother was. By the time we adopted you, you were already living in Germany."

"At this adoption place?" I say. Papa nods. "So why did my Polish mother let me be taken away? That is what I don't understand."

Mama cups her palms around the coffee mug as if she is cold. "We don't know," she says. "All we were told is that she was an unsuitable mother and that it was for the best that you should be adopted. So we chose you and then we brought you home."

"And everything was fine, until she turned up here," says Papa. "We didn't even know that she was still alive. That certainly tore our world apart. We had hoped that you would never find any of this out, but things have changed now. I consulted a solicitor, but to get a restraining order I'd have to know where she is staying here. And I don't."

I picture the woman's thin face and imploring grey eyes and see the cracked leather of her shoes as if she were standing in front of me.

"She can't have seen herself as an unsuitable mother," I say. "Not if she's travelled from Poland to find me and sent letters to this house for all those years. And how come the Red Cross are involved? The letters all had their address on."

Again, that exchange of glances.

"I think that they help people locate their relatives lost during the war," says Papa in a cautious tone. "So I suppose she turned to them first. But we don't know what her motives are, Inge. Our first priority is to make sure that you are safe."

"I don't feel safe," I say, my voice cracking. "And why did you hide the letters from me anyway?"

Mama comes over and puts her arms around me. I lean my head against the crisp white fabric of her blouse and for a moment I wish that I could just rewind a couple of months and never know any of this.

"Because she is not a person to be trusted," she says. "Because we are your parents. Because she will get tired of trying eventually and return to Poland. And Papa and I will continue to bring you up and look after you just as we have always done."

The woman.

"But you haven't *always* had me, have you?" I say. "You have no baby pictures of me."

"We've had you since you were four – for the greater part of your life," says Papa. "We have been here for you and you've had a good upbringing. You can't deny that, surely?"

I can't deny it, so I remain with my head buried in Mama's shirt, but my mind is a whirling mass of thoughts. Although part of me is relieved that this is all out in the open and that perhaps I can try to carry on as before, there are a lot of questions which don't seem to have been answered yet.

"I still think you had no right to hide the letters," I say.

Mama pulls away from me and starts to collect our untouched bowls of soup, the spoons clanging and sliding around inside.

"We had every right," she says. "We were only trying to protect you. Besides, you would not have understood what they said. We didn't know either. Neither of us speaks Polish."

"You must have had some idea," I say. "Or you would have had no need to hide them!"

Mama leaves the room and goes into the kitchen.

"She's upset," says Papa. "It makes her a little brusque, that's all. Everything will be alright. I don't want you to worry."

"You can't carry on trying to keep my birth mother from seeing me, even if what you say is true," I say. "That's not fair on her or on me."

Papa sighs. "And do you think any of this is fair on me or Mama?" he says. "How do you think we feel?"

I feel a flush of shame underneath my sense of injustice. Neither of us speaks for a moment. I fiddle with the tassels on the edge of Mama's pristine white tablecloth and turn a knife over and back again. I can see my face looming large in the blade. Mama's cutlery is always polished to perfection.

"It is best for all of us if she keeps away," says Papa. "Trust me, Inge. You do trust me, don't you?"

Chapter Fifteen

FOR A FEW DAYS, LIFE limps back to normal. Outwardly, at least.

Mama and Papa are very kind to me. They look at me with concern in their eyes and I hear them muttering together at night-time when they think that I am asleep.

But I don't sleep much at the moment. I'm too busy trying to work out what to do next. Wilf's promised to help me in any way that he can. Stefan has said similar, although he has cautiously expressed a little sympathy for my parents too, which is not what I was expecting.

"Whatever has happened, you can't deny that they love you and have given you everything," he says. "They must be hurting and anxious inside, just like you are."

I play these words over in my head when I can't sleep at night.

Maybe Stefan is right. Maybe I should try to see things from their point of view. Perhaps they truly did rescue me from a dreadful place and a mother who was not fit to bring me up.

I want to believe this so much that I find myself squeezing my fists under the covers when I think it. Then I might be able to forget all about the Polish woman and just carry on with my unremarkable, pleasant life.

Part of me is still curious to get to know this woman who must have given birth to me in a tiny village in rural Poland, but at the moment everything about her seems alien and strange to me. I would rather stick with the mama I have known most of my life. Even though she is strict and hard to fathom, she also has a face which sometimes melts with love, and when that happens, it makes up for everything.

So I make a pact with myself to try to forget about the Polish woman, at least for a while.

But the Polish woman does not want to forget about me.

It is a Friday late in June and the weather has burst into full summer bloom. There has been no rain for ages and the front gardens on our close display lawns brown with heat. Everything feels dried up and the sun is so intense that we spend much of our time in the living room with the white blinds lowered.

I drag myself to school every morning with a sense of being stuck in limbo. I haven't worked out how I'm going to look into my adoption further – or how much I want to – and it's so hot that half the time I can't think straight anyway.

On this particular day, although it is only seven o'clock in the morning, there's already a haze of heat shimmering in the air. On the wireless the announcer has just told us that Germany may break weather records today, so I've got a flask of juice in my bag and am wearing my shapeless summer uniform of a blue short-sleeved dress with a zip down the front, and I'm annoyed already that I can feel myself breaking out in a sweat. I'm turning out of the close and heading in the direction of the city centre on my way to school, and I almost walk straight into her.

The shock is so acute that I keep walking, my heart banging.

"Kasia!"

The word pierces right through me.

Somebody's lap. Somebody's voice murmuring in my ear and singing words which tell of another land far away. I am

safe, fiddling with the buttons on the front of her dress.
There's a smell of herbs and of cabbage boiling and a shadowy
presence moving around in the other room of the tiny house
– a man, because I can hear him humming.

My real name is said with such anguish that I stop
dead in my tracks.

I turn round and look her straight in the eye.

"Kasia," she says again, this time in a more gentle tone
of voice. Then in very soft, faltering German: "You…
come home."

I look around. There's no sign of life on the close.

"This is my home," I say, gesturing with one hand to
the rooftop of my house. "If my parents see you, there will
be trouble." It is the first time I have ever spoken to the
woman.

She does not understand what I am saying. She just
shrugs and stares at me with those haunted grey eyes.

I'm at a loss to know what to do. I almost want to run
home again, but I know that Papa will be beyond angry
at the woman this time and I feel a bit sorry for her.
She looks most out of place on our close, in her long grey
dress and headscarf and that same pair of battered leather
shoes.

"Where are you staying?" I say. But it's no good. She
can't understand me. I make a mime of somebody sleeping

by putting my hands together underneath my cheek, but still she does not reply. She just stands there, staring into my eyes until I feel she might be inhabiting my soul.

I take a step towards her. But something makes me stop. She is still so unfamiliar.

"I have to go to school," I say, even though I know she won't understand. "Sorry. It is probably better if you don't come here again."

The woman holds out her thin arms to me, beckoning me into them.

"No," I say, backing away. "You need to leave me alone. I want to carry on my life with Mama and Papa. This is where I live. Do you understand?"

I hear the harshness in my voice and so I turn to avoid what I know will be the hurt and shock in her eyes. I sense them boring into my back as I walk away.

The feeling haunts me for the rest of the day.

It is so hard to concentrate on my lessons after that.

I go to the art room before class, but Wilf isn't there, so I'm not able to tell him what happened.

I can't tell anybody in my class either. A lot of parents are very rude about Polish people and, because they've grown up with this, many of my classmates have the same attitude. I have heard them use the word "Polack", which is an offensive way to refer to poor Polish immigrants.

What would my friends say if I told them that I was the child of a poor Polish woman?

I try to focus on my work, but the way things are, that isn't going to last long.

All I see is the anguished face of the Polish woman. It does not look like the face of a woman who has handed her child over willingly for adoption.

It looks like the face of a woman who has suffered the worst heartbreak imaginable.

And she is my mother. *Matka*.

However much I run this word through my mind, it fails to mean anything. After twelve years being brought up by Mama, I can't think of anybody else really being my mother.

But something unsettled shifts deep inside me. I've seen the glances exchanged by my parents when they think I'm not looking. I've heard Papa muttering on the phone to somebody and asking questions in a low, urgent voice. I see how they both glance outside the front window while we're eating and I hear the false brightness in Mama's voice when she's asking me about what I would like to eat or whether I have done my homework.

Something doesn't add up.

And the only thing I can think of is how to start from scratch with the sums until I get the right answer.

I go looking for Wilf at lunchtime, but one of his classmates tells me he's off sick.

Deflated, I head into the school grounds and sit down with my back against a stout oak tree. I unpack the lunch that Mama has been making me for years. Rye bread, cream cheese and sometimes a bit of smoked fish or sausage, along with a hard green apple and a slab of fruit cake, which she makes every weekend and stores in a square tin in the top cupboard of our neat kitchen.

I'm not hungry today. I pick at the bread, pulling it into dark shreds and dropping it back into the box again. In the end I just eat the apple, wincing at the sour juice on my tongue and chucking most of it, uneaten, into a flower bed next to me.

I've only got one thing on my mind: getting to the truth of how I came to be living in Munich with Mama and Papa. Until I find this out, I can't move forwards with my life.

When I get home, everything is so normal that for a brief, torturous minute, I wonder if I should just block my mind to the images of that Polish woman for ever and try to slip back into my old life.

Papa is outside in the back garden mowing the lawn. I feel a tug at my heart when I see him. He has his old brown cap pulled down over his eyes to shield him from the sun. What am I doing to these good people who have brought me up? The parents who have given me everything for the past twelve years? The mother who dressed me in my school uniform and packed my sandwiches every day, the father who put me on his shoulders and took me to the beach to build sandcastles?

Does it really matter that Mama did not give birth to me in a hospital? Would I ever have such love for a stranger who has turned up and claimed to be my real mother?

But then I remember the hidden letters in the drawer and the way Mama snatched the most recent one off the doormat and hid it, and a little shudder of resentment goes through me.

They stopped me from knowing about my real mother for twelve years.

And I can't help thinking that there is more to their garbled story about adopting me and giving me a better home. I need to work my way through some of the other letters that Mama has been hiding from me all those years.

* * *

On Friday morning I get up an hour earlier than usual. As I go downstairs I see Mama unlocking her desk drawer in the study. She takes out the pile of letters and slips them into the wide pocket of her dressing gown. Then she hears me coming and affects a yawn.

"Couldn't sleep," she says, drawing back the curtains with such force that the painting of Adolf Hitler rattles slightly on its fastening. "These light mornings will be the death of me."

"I couldn't either," I say. "Can we have an early breakfast? I'm starving."

Mama smiles and pushes me into the kitchen. "I'll do your favourite," she says.

She takes some eggs out of the fridge and heats lard in a wide-bottomed frying pan. My stomach leaps with anticipation at the sizzle of the eggs as she drops them into the pan and then spoons the hot fat over the yolks to avoid the soggy white bit which I detest. I watch as she saws her way through one of her handmade loaves and puts two slices under the grill. The tops of those letters are just peeking out from her pocket. I try not to look at them, but it's hard. She is carrying my real mother around in her pocket.

My father comes downstairs about half an hour later and smiles when he sees the empty plates in front of us.

"You couldn't wait for me?" he says. "Is there any sausage?"

With some difficulty, Mama cuts her way through the thick red sausage that she tries to make last all week and tosses it into the frying pan.

It's all so normal that, for about the hundredth time, I question the darkness inside of me and wish that it would just go away.

Papa leaves the table to get ready for the office about ten minutes later. Mama says she is going up for her bath and asks me to wash up. I take the greasy plates over to the sink but I leave them dumped in a pile and quietly follow her, putting all my weight on the banisters so that I don't creak the stairs.

When I get halfway up, I stop. I can see across the landing into Mama's bedroom. I keep very still and watch as she takes off her dressing gown and drapes it across the foot of the bed. Then she remembers. She fumbles for the pile of letters and goes over to the small cabinet next to her bed. This cabinet has a drawer at the top and Mama slides this open and puts the letters inside, but it takes a very long time. I can hear her tugging and pulling at something and then finally, the click of the drawer as she closes it.

So there's another hiding place in this house.

Chapter Sixteen

Saturday.

I wake up from a disturbed sleep. All night I dreamed of the Polish woman with the thin arms and grey eyes. She was trying to get me to go with her somewhere and I could feel her fingers gripping my wrists. We were in a place I didn't recognize, but I knew I was being dragged far away from Mama and Papa and I woke in a cold sweat of fear.

I lie still and let my heart slow down, taking in the familiar surroundings of my bedroom. The red flowers on the curtains which match the flowers on my bedspread. The pine desk beneath the window and the shelves which Papa put up on the wall next to my bed so that I could reach out and take a book to read. Tears spring up in my eyes. I don't want to leave it all. But the fact remains that my parents have lied to me.

And today may be the day I get nearer to finding out the truth.

Papa leaves first.

He's wearing a white shirt and red braces with his usual brown trousers, and he gives off that familiar whiff of shaving lotion and soap as he kisses me goodbye.

Then I wait for Mama to go. I'm trying to look relaxed, so I take a basket of washing out into the back garden and hang it up with the wooden pegs while Mama bustles about finding her shoes and hat and gloves.

"You could give the kitchen a clean later," she says, applying bright red lipstick in the hall mirror and puffing up her blonde curls with her other hand. "Or are you going to see a friend?"

"I might do," I lie.

Mama picks up her brown leather handbag and slings it across her body. She looks a little like a tram conductress but, not for the first time, I can see why Papa fell in love with her all those years ago. Mama has a sort of solid glamour which is wholesome and appealing.

"I'll see you later, Inge," she says. "Don't answer the

door to anybody. You know who I mean by that."

"Yes, yes," I say. "I'll be fine."

Then I watch as she taps out of the close and away into the city.

I give it ten minutes. Then I put the catch on the front door, in case either of my parents come back unexpectedly. I check the back door as well.

Then I go upstairs into the sacred territory of my parents' bedroom.

I don't often enter this room. Mama is not one of those parents who likes her child to burst in on a weekend morning and perch on the edge of the bed. She prefers not to lie in bed, but to get up and get moving, even though I think that Papa would secretly like to sleep in late.

The room is neat and ordered, as are all of our rooms. On Papa's bedside cabinet is a stack of accountancy magazines and a pile of non-fiction books, along with a small green alarm clock and a black spectacles case.

Mama's bedside table has even less on it. There's just a novel with a red leather bookmark sticking out of it.

I guess she keeps everything else in the drawer. The drawer I've been thinking about since yesterday, and where I saw my mother hide those letters.

126

I slide it out as far as it will go. There's no lock on this one, thank goodness.

There are various things in the drawer. Gold necklace chains, some brooches studded with what look like rubies and diamonds and a couple of silver pocket watches which I've never seen before. It all looks valuable, so I guess that Mama inherited them from her wealthy parents who died before I had a chance to get to know them. There are receipts for clothes, a couple of labels snipped out of dresses and a small pot of face cream.

Nothing else.

I run my hand around under the contents of the drawer, but I already know that I couldn't have missed a thick pile of letters.

I sit back on the bed, deflated. Where has she put them now?

I sit and think for a moment.

And then I remember something. The noise coming from the drawer when I heard Mama put the letters away. It sounded as if she was fumbling with something, or pulling something apart and sliding it back again.

I open the drawer again, as far as it can go. I put my hand inside and it hits the back of the drawer pretty quickly. The drawer doesn't seem nearly as deep as the cabinet itself.

I push, at first very gently and then harder, at the back of the drawer. I feel the thin wood start to bend and buckle beneath my hand so I carry on, my heart in my mouth. There's a click and the sides come away. I pull the thin back of the drawer out and gasp. Behind the division is stuffed a small pile of documents, tied up with string. I can see my letters and there are other papers too. With a hand that is now shaking, I pull them out, taking careful note of the way in which they are arranged.

I spread the documents out on the bed.

All the envelopes have the same emblem on them. It's red, and looks like a three-branch tree, with two branches sprouting to the left and one rising straight up in the middle. It is so unfamiliar to me that I stare at it for quite some time, trying to work out what on earth it could be.

The documents inside the envelopes also have the red logo stamped on the top of each one. Some of the pages are forms, filled in by an unfamiliar hand. I start to sift through them and then I get a jolt right through me.

There's a photograph attached to one of them. A faded, tiny, black-and-white photograph of a small girl with fair hair tied into pigtails and wearing a checked dress. She is smiling off to the side and looks about four years old. I pick up that piece of paper and look closely into that girl's face.

The black writing underneath the photograph reads:

```
Birth name: Kasia Pietrowski
Adoption name: Inge Krause
Age: Four years
Height: One metre
Weight: Eighteen kilos
Features: Blonde, blue eyes, of Aryan
complexion
Birthplace: Chodecz, Poland
Lebensborn home: Steinhöring, Bavaria
Date adopted: 13th June 1944
Adoptive parents: Josef and Anneli
Krause
```

Many of the other letters mention my name as well. There is a letter inviting my parents to visit the Steinhöring home and spend an afternoon with me. There is another letter, dated earlier, which includes a list of children's names and descriptions and asks my parents to reply detailing any they might be interested in. My name is among those of several other little children from various parts of Poland.

All of these letters contain that strange red emblem.

I feel sick to the bottom of my stomach.

Mama said that they adopted me from a "centre", but why, then, are there so many other tiny children from Poland listed within these documents? Why had they all been sent so far away from their homes? They can't all have had bad parents who couldn't look after them, can they? I hadn't realized that I was picked out from a long list, as if I were the best chocolate in a box of different soft centres.

I go into my room and get a pencil and notebook. I draw the red emblem and then I copy down the address of the Steinhöring buildings. Then I bundle up the documents and slide them back into the secret compartment at the back of the drawer.

I'm not going to mention my discovery to my parents.

The next part of my journey I will have to make on my own.

I borrow one of Papa's maps from the shelves in his study when he's out in the back garden on Sunday. I take it upstairs to my bedroom and spread it out on the quilt, letting my finger travel across it to where I need to go. I've got an idea that Steinhöring is not too far from where I live because it is listed as being in Bavaria, and when I do find it on the map I can see that it's probably only an hour or so away.

A rush of acid comes up into my chest. I can't believe I'm going to do this. But I already know that I have to. I have no choice. I'm being propelled into this by something I can't see or hear and the only way is forwards.

I need to make a trip.

Because I've been so caught up in my secret research at home, I don't see Wilf until Monday. In any case, he's got a bad cough.

At lunchtime I sneak into the senior pupils' common room. We're strictly not allowed to do that and I get some sharp looks from other pupils as I enter, but I'm past caring whether or not I'm going to get into trouble for anything so unimportant.

Wilf is sitting at one of the square wooden tables with a box of sandwiches in front of him. Senior pupils have privileges, like this common room with its own library and a wide fireplace for cold winter days. They can eat lunch in here and don't have to mix with the rest of the pupils at school.

I slide onto a chair next to Wilf. He doesn't look surprised in the least.

"Hello, beautiful girl," he says. "What's on your mind?"

Wilf always knows when I'm about to ask him

something important, but I'm hoping he won't be too surprised or shocked at what I want from him.

"Wilf…" I hesitate.

"Just say it," says Wilf gently. "Come on. I know you want to ask me something."

"I need you to drive me somewhere," I say. "You can't tell anybody where we're going. Only your father. I need you to promise me that now."

Wilf raises his eyebrows. He's only recently been allowed to drive Stefan's car.

"Are you going to tell me why?" he says, standing up because the bell for the end of lunch is ringing. "Is it to do with your birth mother?"

"Yes," I say. "I'll tell you more after school. I'll come by your apartment, if that's okay."

Wilf drops a swift kiss on top of my head. Several other boys in the common room make derogatory whooping noises. Wilf grins at them, flushing a little, and gives me his shy smile as he leaves the common room.

"See you later," I yell after him. The boys around me laugh, but I don't care.

I will never be embarrassed for loving Wilf.

"You should let me take you both," Stefan is saying. "It

would have to be a Sunday. That's the only day I don't pick up work."

I'm standing in Stefan's small, bare kitchen. There's not even enough room for a table. Just a stove with a rusty kettle on it, an old cream-coloured sink with a wooden board across it for chopping vegetables and a couple of wooden chairs with padded seats.

I look at Wilf. I've explained everything to him and Stefan has heard it all too. And much as I'd feel safer with Stefan driving us to Steinhöring, in another way I don't want to have two people with me when I finally approach that building. I'm not entirely sure I even want Wilf there, which is something that surprises me. But I can't drive, and he can, and I know he'll be gentle and supportive and step back if needed.

"Could we just go on our own?" I ask Stefan. "I don't mean to be rude. But I kind of want to keep this small until I know what I'm dealing with."

Stefan frowns. He glances at Wilf. Something of his paleness has crept back and we can both see that being at school has made him more tired than he's letting on.

"It's an hour's drive, at least," he says. "Are you sure you're up to it, son? And what if they won't give you any information when you get there?"

Wilf leans back in his chair and reaches out an arm to

pull me onto his lap. "For Inge," he says, "I reckon I'm up to it. How can I say no to this girl?"

I bury my face in his neck, feeling shy. "It's true – they might not tell us anything," I mumble.

But inside my heart is thumping like a football against a wall.

I'm going to get to Steinhöring.

I'm going to find out the truth.

I can feel it.

Chapter Seventeen

WE SET OFF ON SATURDAY morning. Wilf picks me up
from the main road round the corner from our close just
after nine. I've been up since five because I couldn't sleep.
Images from my dreams have passed through my head on
a loop since I decided to make this trip.

I've fed Mama and Papa a story about going out into
the countryside for a long walk and a picnic with two girls
from my class at school. I think they've accepted this yarn
because it is something we do occasionally in the summer.
Mama even went so far as to pack me lots of special food
in a hamper, something which makes me feel guilty and
a bit ashamed. I open the hamper after Wilf has lifted it
into the boot of his car, and I gaze down at the red napkins
and cardboard box of potted-meat sandwiches, the slab of

home-made fruit cake dotted with orange peel and plump raisins, and the greaseproof paper containing some of our precious cold sausage, and I realize that Mama has gone to quite a lot of trouble to make sure that I have a good time with my classmates. There's even a glass bottle which smells sharp and sweet when I remove the cork and with another pang I know that Mama has given me some of her precious stock of home-made lemonade.

I slam the boot shut.

I need to focus on what lies ahead.

Wilf and I sit for a moment in the car, looking at one another.

"I love you for this," I say, shyly. We don't often use the word "love". But seeing him sitting there in his father's car, wearing his light brown corduroy jacket because it's not the warmest of mornings yet, his hair falling over one eye and his steady gaze taking me in, I feel a surge of love and security, which is something I need to harness and bring with me on this day.

"I'm already nervous," I say, as Wilf turns the car out of our close and heads away from the city.

Wilf laughs. "Try and rest if you want," he says. "I don't mind. I need to concentrate on where I'm going."

I laugh back. "Fat chance of that," I say. "I'm all wired up. Give me that map and I'll try to navigate."

So I take the battered map and start to trace my finger along our route as we head into the Bavarian countryside. It is not long before we find ourselves amid hills and fields and everything begins to look like a picture postcard of a holiday location.

I wind the window down and take a deep breath of the country air, letting the sun kiss my face for a moment or two. We are now passing through acres and acres of dense woodland.

"This is beautiful," I say. "Mama and Papa must have driven this way when they came to adopt me."

I think of my parents driving along in 1944. Mama would have been wearing a headscarf and dark sunglasses, a slash of red lipstick, and Papa would have had more hair and been driving with one elbow on the window sill, whistling some song or other. What must they have been thinking and hoping on the day they came to collect me and take me home? Were they nervous? Excited? Worried? Had they spent enough time with me on the previous occasion – enough to be sure that, of all the children in the adoption centre, I was the one who would fit in most with their lives and their beautiful home?

Had they argued about which child to adopt, or did they both fall in love with me right away?

"We're here," Wilf says, jolting me back to the present.

He has driven up a wide avenue on a slight hill flanked by trees, and a building has come into view.

He kills the engine and we sit in silence for a moment.

The house is large. It is black and white and reminds me a bit of a Swiss chalet, with a pointed gable and three neat external balconies on the first, second and third floors. Next to it is a separate, smaller detached building with tiny pointed attic windows and a homely look, as if it were a cottage belonging to an elderly couple.

Something about the place makes me want to stay in the car.

I feel as if the building has a personality. I'm getting a strong sense of it as we get out and continue to stare at it.

"I'm not sure about this," I say to Wilf. "I don't know if I want to go any nearer."

Wilf puts his arm around my shoulders. "It's up to you," he says. "But we've come all this way and you won't get another chance for a while. Besides, we may not be able to go inside anyway. It looks like it's a hospital or something."

As if to illustrate his point, a couple of nurses in blue with frilled white aprons and tall hats come out of the front of the house arm in arm and disappear into a car parked just outside.

"Oh," I say. For some reason, I hadn't thought about

what the building might be used for today. My head had been firmly in the adoption centre where I've tried to imagine my four-year-old self waiting, arms lifted, for some kind parents to rescue me.

"Well, we could try," says Wilf. "If we explain why we are here."

We're walking towards the building now. I feel sick to my stomach.

When we reach the black gates I stop.

"That's the emblem," I say, running my hand down the ironwork. Embedded into the middle of each of the front gates, one right, one left, is the tall Y-shaped emblem which was emblazoned all over my adoption papers. There's something else worked into the gates, too. The jagged letters like forked lightning which are still so familiar around Munich.

"SS," I say in a small voice. I glance at Wilf. He's lost his comforting smile.

"We don't know what any of it means yet," he says. "Come on. Let's be brave and ring the bell."

We've nearly reached the black arched front door when something to my right stops me in my tracks.

I go over and stand looking up at a large stone statue of a woman holding a baby. Her left breast is bared, and the baby is latched onto one of them, while she gazes down with tenderness at it. The folds of her dress fall towards the ground, as if they were made of silk and not stone at all.

"What is it?" says Wilf. He has come over to where I'm standing.

"I don't know," I say. And it's true. I stare up into the stone face of the woman and note the way she is looking down at the child. And although there's no wind today, I feel the hairs on my arms standing up and I shiver.

"Are you remembering something?" says Wilf. He takes off his jacket and drapes it over my shoulders.

"I don't know," I say again. And I really don't, but something about the statue is holding my attention far longer than it should do. "It looks as if it's been here a while, though."

The statue is damp with green moss around the base and some of the stone has chipped on the woman's right cheek.

I run my finger across her stone knee, which is the highest point I can reach.

But I *can* reach it. Wasn't there a time when I couldn't? I have some flash of recall, which passes so quickly that I can't grasp it. And then it comes again, slower this time. I'm shorter – tiny. And with my first finger I'm tracing the stone around the base of the statue and craning my neck to stare up at the giant woman and baby looming above me, so high that they seem to block out the sun.

"Yes," I say to Wilf. "Yes. I feel as if I've seen this before. When I was very little."

Wilf follows my gaze. "She looks kind," he says. "So it was a good place, perhaps."

Neither of us look back at the jagged black SS letters worked into the iron gates.

"Perhaps," I say.

"I think we should get this over with," says Wilf. He steers me away from the statue and towards the imposing black front door. "You may find stuff out today. And you may not. But we won't know until we ask."

Wilf reaches out and rings the bell. We can hear it echoing, harsh and sharp, right the way through the building.

I feel as if I'm not connected to the ground. Wilf is half-supporting me, aware that I'm swaying slightly.

"Ready?" he says in my ear.

On cue, the black door swings open and a nurse in a blue dress and white apron appears in the doorway.

"Yes?" she says. "Visiting hours are not until midday, I'm afraid."

"I'm not here to visit a patient," I say, finding my voice with difficulty. "I want to ask somebody some questions about my past."

The nurse steps forward and takes a closer look at me. I know I'm paler than usual. I also know that my face is probably showing fear and tension and the results of a disturbed night.

"What sort of questions?" she says. "I'm afraid we're extremely busy at the moment."

Wilf tightens his grip on my shoulder. I know it's his way of giving me strength and telling me to carry on.

"I think I may have been adopted from here in 1944," I say. Something about saying this out loud makes it feel truly real for the first time. "I'd like to find out why I was here in the first place."

The nurse's face, which had been softening into, if not kindness, then, at least a sort of receptive pleasantness, seems to shrink back into impassiveness.

"I'm sorry," she says. "I really don't know very much about the history of this place. I've only been nursing here for a year. You'd need to write to the director of the hospital with a query like that."

She's about to shut the door in our faces. But I've glimpsed something behind her, towards the back of the building.

"That room," I say, putting my foot in the doorway in a manner which reminds me of the Polish woman when Papa was trying to shut her out of our house. "Could I look at it, please?"

The nurse looks behind, following my gaze, and I use the opportunity to insert myself further into the hallway. Wilf follows me, giving me a quick smile of encouragement mixed with respect. I can be pretty determined when I put my mind to it.

"Come with me then," says the nurse, with a sigh. "But you'll have to be quick. I haven't got time for this."

She leads us into that room at the back of the house.

I walk in with my face screwed into a frown and my eyes taking in the wide windows which run along one side of the room. I look down at the slatted wooden floor, a floor which is now hidden underneath neat rows of hospital beds. I reach down and touch this floor with my finger. Somewhere from deep inside my brain comes the image of a polished pair of black lace-up shoes on the ends of some sturdy legs and, above that, a white dress and apron.

I go over to one of the hospital beds and sit on the edge of it.

"I'd rather you didn't do that," says the nurse. She's looking nervous now, as if her supervisor is about to come in and tell her off.

I ignore her. I feel as if I'm going into some sort of trance. This hospital bed means nothing to me. It's too big – too high, too long – and I don't remember it.

"Cribs," I say out loud, making Wilf jump a little.

And then I see them. A whole line of little cribs draped in a flowery material, where these beds now are, lined up and evenly spaced right across the room. And in the cribs I see the scrunched-up faces of tiny babies who have just been born and I hear the piercing wail of their cries as if I was standing leaning into one of those cots right now.

And there I am. A little four-year-old girl with blonde pigtails, peering into one of them and stroking the face of one of the new babies, before another nurse-type woman in a white apron drags me away gently by the arm and takes me into some other room where there are children the same age as me and she says: "You are not supposed to be in there."

And I don't relate to what she's saying, because it sounds like gibberish to my ear and she is speaking some language I don't understand.

The room spins a little and I grip the edge of the bed with both hands.

Wilf is at my side right away.

"You remember this room?" he says. "That's extraordinary, Inge."

The nurse consults the watch pinned to her uniform and gestures for us to leave the room.

"I'm sorry," she says. "I can't tell you anything and I've got no time to do so even if I could. I really shouldn't

144

have let you come in here at all. You'll need to write to the director if you want any more information."

She ushers us out, but something in her averted eyes and closed face makes me suspicious. I think she knows exactly what went on here and isn't willing, for whatever reason, to tell us.

"Thank you," I say in my most polite voice, the one Mama brought me up to use on every social occasion. "I appreciate you showing us the room."

The nurse gives us a brief nod and closes the front door behind us.

I'm so disappointed that I can't speak.

Chapter Eighteen

WE'RE ABOUT TO LEAVE the grounds of the Steinhöring hospital.

I'm in such a daze that I don't even know which way to head. We pass the statue of the woman and baby again and I don't look at it this time. Wilf guides me towards the edge of the grounds where we've left the car, and then he takes a look at me and steers me instead to a bench just inside the main gates.

"Get your breath for a moment," he says.

We sit for a moment, close together in silence. I look back at the white building with the sloping gates and the black balconies and I feel a heavy weight of depression descend on me. I don't know what I was hoping for today but I knew it was more than this.

"I don't know how I got there," I say, in a voice so desperate that it surprises me. "I know I was adopted. But I don't know how I got there, into that building."

At this point I become aware that somebody else has sat down at the end of the bench, half a metre or so away from me. I glance up, my eyes full of tears. It's an elderly man, with a stick and a long dark coat on, even though it's a warm day. He's regarding me out of the corner of his eye. It's a curious look, as if he's about to say something. I turn away and towards Wilf, but the man clears his throat and somehow I know he's going to speak.

"Where were you born?" he says, taking in my fair hair and skin tone.

"Here," I say automatically. Then I realize. "Well – no. Poland." The words sound so strange coming from my mouth.

"My granddaughter started off in there," he says, glancing back at the building. "She's another one of you. I'm sorry – I couldn't help overhearing what you were saying."

I stare, my manners forgotten.

"What do you mean, 'another one of me'," I say. "One of what?"

The man gives me a considered look. He glances at Wilf, who's leaning forward and looking at him, ready to protect me or move me on at a moment's notice.

"One of Himmler's lot," says the man, in a matter-of-fact voice. "He bred babies in there. Part of Hitler's plan for a master race."

I feel my insides contract. Ahead of me, the black logo of the SS seems to stand out from the gate and move towards me.

"I wasn't bred!" I say. As I say this I am remembering the little cots with the newborns in. So many newborns, all with fair hair and blue eyes. "I was here when I was four."

The man stares at me for a moment. "Yes," he says. "I can see why they'd have brought you here. You look about as Aryan as it gets. Living in Munich now, are you?"

"Yes," I say, although I can't see what business it is of his. Something about his knowing look and his manner is making me feel hot and unsettled.

He edges closer and looks into my face with eyes which speak of knowledge and loss and pain and discovery.

"Polish, huh?" he says. "Like my granddaughter. Except she's not my real granddaughter. She was adopted from here at a young age, just like you. I have come here today for the first time with my daughter. I wanted to see where my granddaughter was adopted from. To try and make sense of it all. "

I'm rooted to the spot now. Behind the man's head the sun's rays shine straight across the stone outline of the woman and baby so that I can't see her features any longer, just the silhouette of her form and the tiny one of the child.

"We're the lucky ones," says the old man. "We have been able to find out what happened. Her birth mother came looking for her."

"So has mine," I whisper. Tears drip down my face, off my chin and onto the ground. I never cry.

The man nods. I see that his eyes, underneath the curiosity, are sad and kind.

"Do you not know how you got here?" he says. His voice is gentler now. He can see my distress. "I do not know if I should tell you. But I can tell you are frustrated at not knowing."

I give a small nod. "Just tell me," I say. "Please. I need to know."

The man reaches out and holds my hand in his, and to my surprise I don't mind him doing so.

"You were stolen," he says. "You are a child of Lebensborn."

I wait. Wilf is holding my other hand and squeezing it hard. The tears are still falling from my chin.

"Himmler came up with the scheme," says the man. "On behalf of Hitler. He opened homes all over Germany. Then he encouraged young healthy German women to sleep with Nazi officers and give birth to pure Aryan children. The babies were brought up in the Lebensborn homes and then farmed out for adoption to German couples, many of them associated with the SS."

"But that's not what happened to me," I say. I am quivering, even though it is not cold today. "I wasn't there as a baby, was I?"

The man sighs.

"Himmler also stole children," he says. "Over a quarter of a million of them from European countries. Most of them were from Poland. My granddaughter came from a tiny village near Poznan."

"How?" I say. "How were we stolen?"

"He used women, often," he says. "They were nicknamed 'The Brown Sisters', because they dressed in brown outfits a little like those of nuns."

A figure looms up in my head and blocks out the sun. My hands reach out to grasp the harsh brown sack-like material of a dress. I can smell the mustiness of the fabric.

"These women went out onto the streets and snatched children who could be passed off as perfect Aryan specimens," he says. "You know – blonde, blue-eyed." He looks again at my face when he says this. "Sometimes the children were snatched right out of their mother's arms," he says, shaking his head. "Sometimes they drugged them."

The cart, with the street disappearing from view as I

watched that tiny figure come out of her house and begin to run after me.

The sting in my arm from the needle. The blackness coming down on me from nowhere.

"They were taken to sorting offices in Germany," says the man. "And then, if they passed a series of tests, they'd be sent to places like this building here and then farmed out to German soldiers and members of the SS who had no children."

"My father was a German soldier," I say. I picture Papa's face and feel a faint twang of homesickness for him – but it's only a pale imitation of what I should be feeling, like it's happening to another girl in another life already.

"What sort of tests?" says Wilf. He's gone as pale as I feel. My hands are gripping his arm.

"To see if the children fit Hitler's idea of the perfect Aryan child," says the man. "They measured faces. Noses. Foreheads. Checked the colour of their eyes."

"What happened to the children who didn't fit?" I say. I'm not sure I really want to hear the answer but I can't seem to stop now.

The man looks down at his feet. "It was not a happy ending for those children," he says. "Camps. Forced labour. Death, often."

"My God," says Wilf softly. "Inge, you could have been one of them."

151

I nod. But there is something bothering me, a question which I'm not sure this old gentleman is going to be able to answer.

"The couples who came here to adopt the children like me," I say. "Did they know that we were stolen from our mothers? Or were they told something different?"

He stands up and adjusts his cap. While I'm speaking, a fair-headed woman of about Mama's age comes out of the building and waves at the old man. "Probably depends who was doing the adopting," he says. "I can't tell you for sure, because I simply don't know if it was the same for everybody. In our case, my daughter did not know that the little girl she adopted was stolen. She was told that the girl had become an orphan, having lost both parents during the war."

He turns to walk away, and then looks back at us huddled together on the bench.

"Good luck, my child," he says. "I hope I did right to tell you. But this war produced too many secrets and lies. I feel a strong desire to tell the truth."

And with that he walks slowly away, leaning on his stick and speaking to himself in a low voice.

"Oh God," I say to Wilf. "Oh God."

And then he holds me while I cry and cry as if my heart will never be mended.

Chapter Nineteen

I DON'T SPEAK FOR THE entire journey home.

Wilf drives, his back tense with worry and his eyes darting sideways to observe me every now and again.

All I can think is the same thing over and over.

I was stolen from my mother.

Oh, my real mother. I have been unfair to her, edging away from her in the street and telling her to leave me alone. And all the time she has been in pain for years, having to live with the fact that I was snatched from her arms and sent beyond her reach.

How long did it take me to bond with my new adoptive parents? Did I cry at night for the first year or did I forget the mother who had given birth to me? Did I miss my life in that little wooden house? Did I miss my friends and the other children in the village?

"Wilf," I say. He jumps a little, because I haven't spoken for nearly an hour and we're almost back home again. "I might have brothers and sisters," I say. "In Poland. I hadn't thought of that."

This is the first positive thought I've had to do with any of this. I always wanted to have a brother or a sister, preferably a younger one who I could cuddle and protect and look out for.

"You might," says Wilf. He looks as bewildered as I feel. "Do you think you should tell your parents about all this now?"

I look out of the window. We've just pulled up on the corner of the street and I can see my house. The large windows and neat flower beds with their pink and white roses and red begonias look like a shoot from a home and garden catalogue. Everything is orderly and in straight lines. There's not a petal on the ground or a patch of grass which looks more worn than any other. And inside that house is Mama, a woman who looks just as neat and in control as the garden.

I swallow. Wilf has killed the engine and we're sitting in silence outside the house now.

"I don't want to go in," I say. "Can I come back to your apartment instead?"

Wilf leans over and kisses me on the forehead. He starts the engine again. "Tomorrow," he says. "You have things you need to ask your parents, yes? And I should not be there when you do it."

"Maybe we should just tell them about you as well," I say. "Get everything out in the open once and for all."'

Wilf comes round to my side of the car and opens the passenger door.

"I don't think that's going to help you right now," he says. "They'll just get angry and try to stop me seeing you. I love you and I want to be around for you. It's important."

I give him a small smile. As ever, Wilf is speaking a lot of sense.

"Thank you," I say, reaching up to kiss him. "For taking me today and for being there. I don't think I could do any of this without you."

I watch as he gets into the car and my heart hurts a little.

Wilf had the worst start to life imaginable. But he has Stefan. He has a birth father who loves him and looks out for him and who he can come home to at the end of every day. And until recently, I thought I had all this too.

But my real mother is somewhere in this city, trying to find ways to reach me. She is small and lost and in a foreign country, just like I was when I arrived on a train and was placed in Steinhöring.

What must she have gone through after I was snatched away from her? What did she do? How did she find me, twelve years later? I guess she's been sending letters to the Red Cross for many years.

How will we ever talk together when she only speaks the barest bit of German and I don't know any Polish?

I must find her again.

All these thoughts crowd my head as I walk slowly up the path towards the house. I stop outside for a moment, trying to calm myself down and somehow find strength for what lies ahead. I feel as if I left home this morning aged sixteen and have come home with my childhood finished for ever.

I let myself in the front door and go into the kitchen.

Mama turns around from where she's cutting fat and sinew off a thin piece of meat at the sink. The smell makes my stomach turn.

"What is that?" I say. I'm trying hard to appear normal, which makes my voice sound oddly neutral and, sure enough, Mama gives me a frown.

"Are you alright, Inge?" she says. "Didn't your picnic go well? It's a rabbit, in answer to your question. That's just what the butcher happened to have in this morning."

"Oh," I say, putting the empty picnic hamper on the table and starting to unload the plates and cutlery for washing. "Yes. The picnic was good, thanks. My friends liked the food."

In fact, Wilf has taken the entire picnic home in his haversack to enjoy with Stefan later. I couldn't even face the lemonade, let alone the bread and meat.

"My fruit cake turned out very well this time," says Mama. "I'm glad you all enjoyed it."

I feel a little twinge of guilt when she says this. She did go to a lot of trouble. But I tell myself that I need to stay strong. There are things I am going to have to ask and I don't want to crumble before I've even started. It would still be so easy to go into denial mode and just pretend that none of this has happened, carry on as normal with school and homework and eating and seeing Wilf and just stay Inge Krause for the rest of my boring, unremarkable and safe life.

But I need to be true to what I feel inside. And inside, I am starting to feel just a little like Kasia.

Kasia Pietrowski.

Chapter Twenty

"Papa will be home for supper at seven," says Mama.

She is throwing a handful of chopped rabbit into sizzling fat. The sweet smell of the flesh cooking makes me want to gag and I'm relieved when she throws in an onion three minutes later and the smell takes on a savoury tang instead.

Papa comes home on the dot of seven. He sits down at the dining table, rubbing his hands in anticipation of Mama's cooking as he always does, even when the meal served up is not quite worthy of the hand-rubbing. I sit down, looking at Papa's green knitted sleeveless jumper and white shirt and his brown capable hands and I remember those hands swinging me round and round when I was a little girl and the love that shone from his eyes and all I can think is: *I don't know who my real papa is.*

Thinking that way about Papa makes me too sad to eat. I keep looking at Mama and Papa and remembering things from my childhood. All the outings we went on, all the birthdays and Christmases, the holidays and the meals around this very table.

We eat in companionable silence, or at least my parents do. Papa is flicking through the evening paper and Mama eats her food with care and neat precision, leaving nothing on her plate and lining her knife and fork up like a pair of straight legs, knees together. I play around with the rabbit stew but very little reaches my mouth. Underneath my mask of a face, my heart is in turmoil and my stomach is shooting up little skeins of sourness. I feel dried out, sick, like I'm coming down with a bad cold or something.

I wait until Mama's cleared away the plates and made coffee for her and Papa and then I push away my glass of juice and take one deep, steadying breath. Then I say: "I didn't go for a picnic today."

Mama looks at me, waiting. Papa puts down his newspaper and removes his glasses.

"I went to Steinhöring," I say. Just like that. I can't stop myself now, even if I want to. This stuff has been building up and building up and I'm going to have to go on the ride with it, wherever it might take me.

"Steinhöring?" says Papa. I notice he hasn't looked at Mama. "Whatever for, pumpkin?"

"I went to find the Lebensborn home," I say. My voice sounds flat and chilly.

Mama pushes back her chair with a violent scraping noise and gets up without a word. She goes into the kitchen and closes the door. I didn't expect that. So Papa and I sit there for a moment, looking at one another and wondering who is going to speak first. In the end it's Papa.

"You went there on your own?" he says. "It's quite a way. How did you get there?"

"With my friend," I say. "She borrowed her mother's car to take me."

"Go on," says Papa. "Say what you've got to say." I notice he's lost some colour in his face.

"Why didn't you tell me that's where you got me from?" I say. "The other night. When we spoke about me being adopted. Why didn't you mention it?"

Papa leans forwards and takes my hands in his own warm ones. "We didn't think you needed to know, Inge," he says.

"That's not my name," I say. "That's not my name. That's the name you gave me, but it's not my name."

I sound so calm and controlled that I'm beginning to frighten myself. I can see the damage I'm doing to my dear

Papa who is sitting right in front of me and holding my hands, but I can't stop now.

"How did you find out?" says Papa. "About Steinhöring?"

Mama comes back into the room at this point. Her face is white and I notice that her hands are shaking as she sits down at the table again.

"Sorry," she says. "It was a bit of a shock hearing you mention that place. We had no idea that you knew anything about it."

"I didn't," I say. "Until I found your secret drawer upstairs."

Mama's face tightens. "You had no right to go through my private possessions," she says. "I thought I brought you up better than that, Inge."

I see a flash of red and realize that I'm so angry that my body is starting to tremble.

"And you had no right to hide the truth from me," I say. "I had to find out from a complete stranger today. Did you know that I was stolen off the streets in Poland?"

I watch my parents' faces very carefully. Mama betrays no emotion, other than the deadly white hue of her skin. But Papa's eyes are full of tears. He blows his nose on one of his white handkerchiefs with his initials sewn in blue on the corner.

"Of course not," says Mama, before he has a chance to

161

161

answer. "We were just told that you needed a good home. And we've given you that, haven't we? A home and twelve years of love. Isn't that what counts?"

I'm standing up now. I hold onto the back of my chair because my legs have lost all their strength and I feel dizzy.

"No!" I shout. "It's not what counts. What counts is the truth. And I don't believe you. I think you're lying to me. I think you knew full well where I'd come from, and how. The old man said that we were farmed out to families of German soldiers. You're a German soldier, Papa. You must have known what was going on in Poland. You must have known what Himmler was planning to do."

My voice is so loud that Mama covers her ears. Tears are falling down her face now too. Papa reaches out to her but she pushes his hand away.

"We love you, Inge," she says, in a voice cracked with anguish. "We will always love you."

But I ignore the sentiment. "You're lying," I say. "You knew I'd been stolen. You knew. I can see it in both your faces. I'll never forgive either of you for this. Never."

I push the chair so hard that it knocks a cup off the table and china smashes on the parquet floor. Neither of my parents move.

I leave them sitting there at the dining table. I leave my old life sitting there in ruins. And I go upstairs with my heart pounding and my hands trembling and I sit on the bed and let the tears fall and fall until I am exhausted.

Later that night, Mama creeps into my bedroom and sits on the edge of my bed. I pretend to be asleep but I think she knows I'm fully alert.

"Inge," she whispers. "We're sorry, both of us. I know what it looks like. But we really didn't know anything other than that we couldn't have children of our own, and you were so beautiful and in need of a new home, so that's why we brought you back here. Does it really matter so much how you got here? Surely we can forget about the past now? Try to move on as a family?"

She pushes a strand of hair back from my face. I lie as still as possible even though her touch is making me shudder and I want to slap her hand away from me.

She waits for a moment, then sighs and moves away from the bed.

I open one eye. I watch my adoptive mother walk slowly back into the hallway as if her heart is breaking. I feel as if my heart might be breaking too. I can feel the sadness coming off her, see it in the way that she's moving. I know that our relationship will never be the same again now.

It is impossible for us to get back to where we were.

Chapter Twenty-one

THAT NIGHT I DREAM.

The woman's grip on my arm is as rough as ever. Her voice is like poison in my ear. But this time I am grabbed by other arms too and bundled into a rough blanket which is pulled right over my face so that I fumble and pull at it in a panic.

My bones jolt about on the floor of a cart.

There is a sharp scratch in my arm, like a beesting.

Then the cart begins to travel away.

I am on the cart. I can feel the horses dragging me in the opposite direction from everything I have ever known and loved. I pull the blanket off my head and stand up in the back of the cart on my sturdy child's legs and grip the wooden flap at the back so that I can stare down the village street towards what used to be my home. I somehow know that in less than a minute I am going to be asleep, so it seems important that I should look and remember as much as I can.

And then I see her. A small figure in a headscarf coming out of one of the tiny grey houses at the side of the road, shielding her eyes from the sun with one hand and staring after the cart as it gathers speed. Then it's like something dawns on her and she begins to run after us, except that we are going too fast for her now and she is left behind almost straight away, a tiny dark dot zigzagging erratically like a fly on a street in a small village, set against a background of fields and hills and trees which loom larger as the houses shrink away.

"Matka!" I scream from the cart as I watch everything I've ever known and love disappear behind me.

But it is no good.

Something is making my vision blur and shake at the edges.

I am pushed down onto the floor of the cart.

And that is when everything stops.

* * *

When I wake up the next morning there can be no going back to my old life.

I sit on the edge of my bed for some time. I look down at my hands, my legs, my feet and they look different this morning. The first person who ever saw them was a woman in Poland – my real mother. It was she who held me as a baby and sang to me at night. It was she who dried my tears and held my hand and dressed me every morning. And it was she who watched in shock and anguish as I was snatched off the street by one of Hitler's Brown Sisters to begin the long journey which would see me end up in Munich.

Matka.

She is my mother. And she's out there in the city somewhere, thinking that I have rejected her.

I go over to Wilf's that afternoon.

Wilf blows out his cheeks and makes a long sigh, his eyes upon my face.

"Guess you've had the discussion then," he says.

I go into the tiny kitchen and unwrap the two pieces of coffee cake that I've stolen from Mama's kitchen. I can tell by the way the knife sticks that the cake is not at its freshest, but I need a sugar fix so I finish cutting it anyway and make two weak cups of coffee to go with it.

We sit on the kitchen chairs and eat the cake. Then Wilf takes my hand in his.

"So did they admit it?" he says. "That you were stolen?"

I put my plate in the sink and move my chair around to where he's sitting so that we can be close. Then I tuck my head onto his shoulder and he rests his cheek on top of my head and we just sit like that for a long while, without speaking.

"They didn't admit it in so many words," I say. "But they didn't deny it either, which tells me everything I need to know. They just said that it wasn't important how they got me, only that they got me at all."

Wilf puts his arm around my shoulders and turns my chin with his hand so he can look into my eyes. "You know, in a way they're right about that," he says. "You can't deny that they've given you a good life." I can almost see him visualizing Mama's luxury kitchen.

I know he's right. But his comment sends up a protest inside me.

"But it started with dishonesty," I say. "They hid the truth from me. They knew where I'd come from. They hid the letters from my Polish mother for all those years.

So the life I've been living here just feels like one big lie."

Wilf drains his coffee with a slight grimace. "So what are you going to do?" he says. "You know I'll help you, whatever it is."

I give him a small smile. "I guess I need to get out there and look for my birth mother."

I look at Wilf, at his kind eyes and worried expression. "I do love you," I say. "I'm glad every day that I've got you in my life."

Then I can feel myself blushing, so I get up and wash up the plates. I feel naked and vulnerable when I talk about loving Wilf. But at the moment, all my emotions are heightened, on edge, and it's making me feel a deeper sort of connection to him.

"I should get home," I say. I lean up to kiss him. I like the way that his height makes me feel small and protected.

I run my hand down his thin back while we hug. I look into his eyes. They crinkle up when I'm near, the warmth and spark travelling from his eyes into my own.

"Do I still look German?" I whisper. "Do I still look like the same girl you asked out?"

Wilf smooths my hair back from my face and cups my cheeks in his hands. I love Wilf's hands. They are thin, with long, beautiful fingers which look as if they should be stroking the keys of a piano.

"You look no different to me," he says. "You are still the girl I fell in love with."

I feel tears pricking at my eyes and give a sniff. Wilf puts his hand on the back of my neck and pulls my head forwards for one gentle kiss on the lips.

Then he gives me his warm smile and I head home.

I spend the rest of the afternoon in my bedroom. I need to plan what to do next.

Chapter Twenty-two

I HAVE NO IDEA HOW or where to start looking for my Polish birth mother.

I don't know whether she is nearby, or whether she's even still in Munich. Stefan said that to get here from her part of Poland would have been a journey fraught with uncertainty and danger, due to many borders still being closed. So I don't know whether she will even attempt to return to Poland, or if she will be allowed to remain in Germany without a job. And I have no idea, after the awful way I've treated her, if she will now want anything to do with me. I feel really ashamed when I think of how I snapped at her and tried to cut her dead.

The Nazis stole me from right underneath her nose and sent me to a foreign country and a building full of strangers. She has lived all these years trying to find out the truth. And the horrors of that truth affect me now, as badly as they must have affected her.

But she is still a stranger to me. I can't remember much of what it felt like to be a small child playing on the streets of Chodecz. And that's why I feel sick and scared when I think about the future. After everything that has happened at home, there's no way that I am going to have a happy-ever-after with Mama and Papa, even if I did my very best to forget my past and try to revert back to the life I had before. Deep down, I would always know that they adopted me in the knowledge that I had been stolen from my mother and that they did nothing about it other than hide the evidence from me for twelve years.

So for a few days I drift, feeling disconnected from everybody and in neither one place nor another. I can't go back to how I was before. But I've not arrived yet in the place I think I might need to be. So I feel weightless, ungrounded. At home I walk around as if I am sleepwalking. Mama and Papa give me anxious glances, but there's very little that they can say to me at the moment so we mainly exist in a tense, terse silence. It makes me feel tired, and scared, and sad for everything I've lost and will lose.

None of us can find the words to make anything better.

* * *

I spend an intensive week looking for the woman who I know to be my mother. It is difficult, because I have to fit it all in around my lessons at school.

I walk into the city centre of Munich and wander about for hours, searching, staring. I observe people sitting outside cafes, even though I know she will not be able to afford the prices of post-war coffee and cake. I go into the library, even though I know she will not be able to read most of the books in there. I go into churches, having no idea at all whether she is religious. I pace around the old town and sit in Marienplatz for a while, watching people go by and wishing that I could see her small, thin form coming towards me.

But of course I do not find her. Now that I am looking, she will not be found. All I have of her are the letters upstairs in Mama's drawer which she no longer bothers to try to conceal from me, and my memory of her holding her arms out towards me.

And I rejected her.

I take to praying up in my bedroom at night. I don't know who I'm praying to. This has never been a household with religion at its fore. Stefan and Wilf have no belief in God either. After what happened to them during the war and in the camps, I can't blame them. But I whisper to God, or whoever is up there, to please send my real mother back to me so that I can at least tell her I am sorry for ignoring her over the past few weeks.

And I have no belief in these prayers actually working. I just say them to make myself feel as if I am at least doing something, even if it's only from my bed in the middle of the night.

Chapter Twenty-three

"WHAT WOULD A POOR POLISH woman do over here?"
I say.

I am sitting on the floor at Wilf's feet.

"Sorry?" says Wilf. I've got my head on his knee and
I'm in a reflective mood.

"Presumably she'll need to be working," I say. "To earn
money to be able to stay here. So what would she do?"

Wilf shrugs.

"Cleaning," says Stefan, coming out of the kitchen
with a dish of boiled potatoes and putting it on the
small brown table behind us. "And supper's ready, such as
it is."

I unfold myself and follow the smell of the food.
"That's not a great job, is it?" I say, helping myself to a

large spoonful of black beans and sprinkling them over the pie that Stefan has made.

Stefan smiles at me over the top of his glasses. "It's a job," he says. "And for somebody who does not speak our language and who is desperate to stay in this country, it is a godsend. What else could she be employed as?"

We sit in silence for a moment but none of us can come up with anything.

I smile back at Stefan. "You're brilliant." I say, "that must be it."

"Ach," says Stefan. "You've got plenty of common sense of your own, Inge."

I feel a bit choked at the use of my old name, but it still sounds right coming from Stefan, so I let it go.

After supper we trawl through Stefan's phone book and find the name of four domestic agencies in town which supply cleaners.

"Will you come with me?" I ask Wilf. But I already know the answer.

Wilf accompanies me to the first agency in town. It has a very sleek interior and is staffed by women with immaculate blonde hair and dark-blue uniforms sitting behind heavy oak desks.

"Yes?" says one of these women. "Can I help you?"

There's some doubt in her voice. I guess we don't much look like people who need to hire a cleaner. Wilf is wearing his faded brown cord jacket and I've still got my school uniform on because it didn't occur to me to change.

"We're trying to trace somebody who might be working for you," I say.

The woman looks even more doubtful at that. "We can't give out any confidential information," she says. "Sorry."

She doesn't sound sorry in the slightest. She sounds as if she wants us to scuttle off and stop soiling the blue patterned carpet beneath our feet.

"So if we gave you a name you wouldn't tell us if she worked for you?" says Wilf. "Even if it's an emergency?"

"Sorry," says the woman. "I'm not allowed to do that, I'm afraid."

She holds our gaze until it seems obvious that there's no point continuing the conversation. Besides, looking around the agency, I find it hard to believe that they'd hire anybody who looked like my mother.

"That's an agency for posh cleaners," I say as we leave. "They probably all have to wear those hideous blue suits as well."

Wilf laughs and propels me down a couple of side streets towards the next agency.

This one has a different feel from the moment we push open the wooden door. For a start it's very dark in here. There are no oak desks or women with blonde hair, only a harassed-looking middle-aged man in a brown suit shouting into the phone in a language I don't recognize.

We wait for the man to finish his conversation and he throws the phone down, wiping sweat from his brow and gesturing for us to sit down on two plastic chairs.

"Sorry," he says, sweeping his hair to one side and leaning back. "I deal all day with foreigners. It can be very stressful."

Wilf and I exchange glances. A little thrill of hope shoots up inside my chest.

"We're trying to find a woman who we think may be cleaning for your agency," says Wilf, without preamble. That's what I love about Wilf. He's very good at getting straight to the point when necessary.

"Yes?" says the man. "We're not supposed to give out personal information." He glances at a card index on his desk when he says this. I see Wilf take it in.

"Not to worry," he says. "Do you have many Polish people come for jobs here?"

The man laughs. It is not a happy sound. "More than

there should be," he says. "The war's sent them all in search of a better life here. I doubt they're going to find it."

"Indeed," says Wilf, giving the man a conspiratorial smile. Then he frowns, puts his hand on his chest and gives a cough which frightens me with its rattle. "Sorry," he says. "It's probably the heat. I haven't been very well."

I glance at him in alarm. Then I see the look in his eye. "I haven't got your medication with me," I say. "Just sit still for a moment. Breathe."

Wilf is coughing again, with one hand held out in apology. The man in the brown suit has leaped up, unsure what to do.

"Let me get you a glass of water," he says. "Come with me. The kitchen's out the back. You're in charge of the shop, young lady."

Wilf gets up, still bent over coughing, and follows the man out of the office.

I'm on it. Quick as anything, I've swiped that box off the desk and am flicking as fast as I can through the cards in the index files. I shoot straight to "P" for Pietrowski and fumble my way through until I see what I'm looking for. There it is. Pietrowski. Mrs Kristina Pietrowski. I pause as I take in her full name.

With a trembling hand, I grab a pen from the man's desk and copy the addresses and the information I need down onto the only thing I have – the palm of my hand. I'm shoving the box back into position when Wilf comes back through from the kitchen holding a glass of water and wearing a sheepish expression.

"I'm so sorry to have troubled you, sir," he is saying to the man, who appears to have gone three shades paler. "You've been very kind."

"Don't mention it," says the man. "Thought I was going to have a corpse in my office for a moment there! You should get a doctor to look at that cough."

Wilf takes my hand and pulls me out of the agency, still smiling apologetically at the man.

"Did you get it?" he says.

"Yes!" I say. I squeeze his hand.

"Let's find her then," he says.

Chapter Twenty-four

WE SIT IN THE STREET and look at the information scribbled onto my hand – all the places where Mrs Pietrowski cleans.

I start in surprise.

"The daughter of this woman, Mrs Schmidt, is at our school," I say. "Seriously."

"Really?" says Wilf. "That's amazing. Do you know her?"

I grimace. "It's Marta. I've got absolutely nothing in common with her."

"Well, you have now," says Wilf. "Although not much. Isn't she that anti-Semitic girl who doesn't like me?"

We sit in silence for a moment. I'm chewing over the best thing to do next.

"I'm going to have to go and speak to her," I say. "But I can't do anything until school tomorrow."

"You could go straight to her house," says Wilf. "We've got the address now. And it says that Mrs Pietrowski cleans every afternoon from two until five."

I'm tempted. Very tempted. But the thought of turning up at an unfamiliar house and possibly causing a fright for my real mother, or being turned away by Marta's mother, prevents me from rushing over.

"No," I say. "I'll wait until tomorrow."

Wilf nods.

We walk home hand-in-hand in silence.

Marta Schmidt.

I think about her for the rest of the evening.

She's anti-Semitic, for a start. She's sneered at my Wilf for being Jewish. That makes my blood boil every time I even look at her.

I sigh as I lie on my bed staring up at the ceiling. It's so typical that it would be somebody like Marta. A girl I've barely said two words to. She's part of a group of girls who tend to ignore me most of the time, apart from when they're teasing me about Wilf.

It occurs to me that I could just hang around outside

Marta's house and see if my mother arrives for work. But I would hate to be seen by Marta or her mother and then have to answer a whole load of questions. So I decide, reluctantly, that I should approach Marta and ask if I can visit her house.

The next morning I go and find Wilf at first break, for courage.

He's sitting in a scruffy armchair with his brown scarf wound around his neck, immersed in a small leather-bound book.

"Are you alright?" he says when he looks up and sees me.

Wilf feels like the only constant in my life at the moment. For one dizzying moment I imagine what it would be like not to be able to speak to him any more and the air around me seems to spin and grow faint.

I perch on the edge of his chair. "I am now that I can see you," I say. That is true. There's always a sense that the world stops moving and grounds itself when I see Wilf.

"Let me know if you want me to come with you after school," says Wilf. "Assuming that Marta lets you visit."

I frown. "She's not the friendliest," I say. "And I think I'd better go on my own to this one."

"Good point. She's not going to want to see me at her house, is she?"

We gather up our school books and part in the long grey corridor outside.

"Good luck," says Wilf as he walks away. "I will be thinking of you."

And that is one thing I can believe in, so I smile and hug my books to my heart as I head into my next lesson.

Why is it that whenever you are waiting for something important, time never seems to get faster but slows down, so that every moment leading up to it is weighted with a sort of heavy clarity and you wish that you could grab time by a handle and speed it up a bit? I sit through the lesson and although my pencils skim over the top of an exercise book, I have no recollection of what I've written, or why. My head is full of only one thing. It dominates all other thoughts and pushes them away every time they try to break through. And if I ever do manage to let my mind wander just for one moment to something different, I get a feeling a bit like being punched in the stomach and I almost want to bend over as if I've been winded, for the feelings are so intense and sharp that I can hardly bear it.

I wonder what my mother's thinking. If she's thinking of me, still.

The lesson finally ends and we're sent back into our own classrooms for a session with our form teacher. She's telling us about a competition that the school is running, but I'm not taking in a word. I focus my gaze on the back of Marta's shiny black hair and rehearse what I'm going to say to her.

After twenty minutes we're released for the next lesson and I seize my chance as we're walking in the direction of the science lab.

"Marta!" I say, catching up with her. The girls with Marta raise their eyebrows and look at me with disdain.

"Are you talking to me?" says Marta, although it's pretty obvious that I am.

"Can I have a word in private, please?" I say, trying to keep my voice firm and friendly. "It won't take too long."

Marta's cronies melt away into the background, giggling.

"Spit it out, then," says Marta. Not for the first time, I wonder how some people can be so rude.

"Okay," I say. "This will sound really strange. I need your help. It's important."

"You need my help?" says Marta. "What could I possibly help you with? I don't even know you."

I take a steadying breath. She's already annoying me. "My mother wants to hire a new cleaner," I say. I've been giving this some thought. I can't trust Marta with the real reason I want to meet her cleaning lady. So I came up with this one in the dead of night. "And she wondered if I can come and meet yours?"

Marta stops and stares at me. "Why can't she come herself?" she says. "Or just go to an agency like everybody else does?"

"She's too busy," I say. "And we're desperate for a new cleaner."

I'm not sure Marta's going to swallow this, but I forgot that she's not particularly clever.

"I always thought you were a bit strange," she says. "Now I know for sure."

I force a smile. She's not making this easy. "Could I come today?" I say. "Would you ask your mother, please?" I keep my voice firm and low, in the hope that the seriousness will impress her.

Marta is shaking her head. "You're crazy," she says. Then she sees my face. "Oh, alright," she says. "I'll ask her. Wait for me at the school gates at four. And cheer up, for God's sake."

Then she heads off to the science lab, still shaking her head.

* * *

I drift through double biology with no sense of what's going on around me. All I can think of is what I'm going to say to my mother when I finally see her. I'm aware I haven't been kind and I feel full of guilt for that. I keep trying to imagine what it must be like working as a cleaner in a foreign country far from home, and I can see that it must take some courage.

Four o'clock finally rolls round. As I wait for Marta's mother at the school gates, as arranged, I get a little thrill of nerves in my stomach. I've never been inside any of the houses belonging to the seriously rich girls in our school. I'm aware that I may be entering a new world.

Marta walks past me without saying a word and goes towards a silver car. I see her bend over and talk with her mother. At one point they both turn and look over at me, and then the conversation continues.

Marta's mother slides her elegant legs out of the car, pushes her sunglasses onto the top of her head and walks towards me.

"Hello," she says, holding out her hand. "Inge?"

I'm almost tempted to say no but I shake the proffered hand.

"I gather that you'd like to come and speak to my cleaner?" she says. Her voice is neutral, so I can't tell what she's thinking. But she does not have the harsh manner of her daughter, so I try to take heart from that.

"Yes, please," I say. "My mother is looking for a new cleaner and we have heard that yours is a very good one."

Marta's mother smiles. "She certainly is," she says. "Although she speaks hardly any German. But luckily I speak some Polish. So we get by."

As she says this, I see the depth in Mrs Schmidt's eyes. There is something wise about her, something measured. I realize that her daughter may resemble her physically, but that is where the similarity ends.

"You are welcome to come home with us now," she says. "I presume you've cleared it with your parents?"

"Yes," I say. "They know I'm out after school today."

"Okay," says Mrs Schmidt. She's shepherding me towards the silver car as we speak. I slide into the back seat, admiring the smell of leather and the cleanliness of the interior. Marta glares at me from her seat in front. She says nothing at all but I can feel the resentment coming off her.

We drive for only five minutes and then Marta's mother leans out of the car, punches a code into a metal box and two black wrought-iron gates swing open ahead of us. I have a hard job not letting out a gasp when I see Marta's house. It sits at the back of a perfectly-gravelled circular drive, surrounded on either side by lawns, richly blooming rose beds and, on one side, a tennis court.

"Yes," says Marta's mother, watching my expression in her driving mirror. "We have a nice lifestyle, I suppose. My husband is a successful man."

She says this with little feeling in her voice. Marta laughs from the passenger seat.

"We're rich," she says. "We can buy anything we want. You should see my bedroom."

Mrs Schmidt ignores her daughter, but again she catches my eye in the mirror and I swear I see a glimmer of warmth in them.

We climb out of the car and walk towards the house. "You'd better behave yourself," Marta says as her mother inserts a key into the polished wood of the front door. The house is almost colonial in style, with grand pillars and an enormous porch. The windows shine as if they're cleaned every day.

A woman in a blue dress and white apron comes towards us down the hall with a disapproving look on her face.

"I didn't know you were bringing a guest, Mrs Schmidt," she says.

Marta's mother smiles and waves me through into a vast kitchen. "Spur of the moment decision," she says.

I try not to look too impressed at the kitchen, which makes Mama's state-of-the-art version look small in comparison.

"That's our cook," says Marta in a sniffy voice, although it's pretty obvious, as the woman has returned to a chopping board in the middle of the room and is slicing up some sort of meat. I can't help noticing the quantity. There's enough meat there to feed a family of four for several weeks. Marta's mother must have some special connection to a local butcher. We never get this much meat at home.

"Help yourself to juice," says the cook, tilting her head towards a giant white fridge-freezer in the corner. "Marta. Get your guest a glass."

Marta drags her feet to the cupboard and pulls out a couple of glasses.

I pick up the glass of orange juice which Marta bangs down in front of me and take a cautious sip. It's freshly squeezed, not like the concentrated stuff that we have at home. I can feel shreds of orange inserting themselves between my teeth.

Marta's mother throws her bag and keys down onto the massive granite workstation in the middle of the kitchen, goes over to the door and shouts, "Kristina! Could you come downstairs, please?"

I feel panicked. I didn't realize this was going to happen straight away.

Marta's mother stands in the doorway with her hands on her hips, looking in the direction of the stairs. Marta is eating cake at the kitchen table but keeping one beady eye on my face. I hear soft footsteps creeping down the steps, and I get the now-familiar shot of adrenalin up from my stomach towards my head. Because of where Marta's mother is standing, at first I don't see the woman coming into the room and I'm actually offering up a prayer in my head which goes like this: *Please let me know what to say. And let her be glad to see me.*

And then she is standing in front of me.

Her eyes widen and then one hand creeps up over her mouth. She looks from me to Marta to Marta's mother again, with a questioning look in her grey eyes.

"Go ahead," says Mrs Schmidt. "Sit at the table if you like. I can see that you'd probably like to ask Kristina some questions, Inge. If you want me to stay then I can translate."

I laugh inwardly. I certainly do have some questions. But not the ones that anybody is expecting me to ask.

Kristina comes over to the table and sits down so that we are facing one another across it. She reaches out and takes my hand and for the first time, I don't resist her, even though it feels odd to have a stranger holding it. Then, in a faltering tone of voice, she speaks.

"Daughter," she says. "You come to find me, yes?"

I'm so surprised to hear her speaking these words in German that tears dart up into my eyes and for a moment I can't compose myself enough to speak.

Mrs Schmidt is staring at me, a frown on her face. She gestures at her cook to leave the room. "Marta," she says to her daughter. "Go upstairs and make your bed. Your room is a disgrace."

Marta seems about to protest, then takes one look at her mother's face and leaves the room without a word.

"Inge," says Mrs Schmidt. "Kristina seems to think that she's your mother. Is this true?"

I nod. "Yes," I say. "She is my *Matka*."

At that word, the lined, brown face of my mother comes alive and she grips my hand harder across the table.

"Yes," she says. "*Matka. Matka.*" And she points at herself with a wide smile that I have never seen before. Even Marta's mother is smiling at this moment, a smile quite different to the one she put on when I arrived. She sees me looking and tries to compose herself, but it's too late.

"Oh my God," she says. "Now I know why you have come here today. Yes, I can see it. You have the same eyes and the same nose."

She goes over to the sink and fills up the kettle. I am looking into the grey-flecked eyes of my mother and for the first time, I give her a hesitant smile.

"My name is not Inge," I say to Marta's mother. "My name is actually Kasia."

At this, my wrist is gripped even harder.

I want to ask the question that has been haunting me in my dreams.

"Mrs Schmidt," I say. "Could you please ask Kristina if she knows who stole me?"

"Stole?" says Marta's mother, sitting down at the table. "What on earth are you talking about?"

"It's a long story," I say. I feel very tired. I long for Wilf to come and put his arms around me. I'm craving the familiar all of a sudden. I look at Kristina's face and realize that I really don't know her at all. And Marta's mother, however kind, is still a stranger.

She is speaking in Polish to Kristina now. It is strange to hear the language coming from her mouth. I wait, watching Kristina's face. I see shadows pass over it, again and again. I see her shake her head in anguish at one point. Then she replies to Mrs Schmidt in a low, urgent tone, glancing at me the whole time.

Marta's mother listens, her face losing colour. Then she reaches over and takes my hand.

"She found out in a newspaper," she says. "She saw an article about the Red Cross and the work they do. It mentioned the Lebensborn programme and how Himmler sent women to steal Polish children and she realized that this was what happened to you. So she wrote to you via the Red Cross for years, but there was never any reply."

I picture the fat wad of letters in Mama's drawers and tears rise up into my eyes.

"Please tell her that Mama never let me have the letters," I whisper.

Mrs Schmidt relays the information. Kristina nods and mutters something back.

"She suspected that," says Marta's mother. "She says she cannot blame your mama. She would probably have done the same in that position."

I realize that I'm crying, because fat tears are dripping into the mug of coffee that Marta's mother has just put in front of me.

"They stole me," I whisper. Marta's mother relays this to Kristina. "They stole me from you." My tears are flowing freely now and I'm past caring.

Kristina reaches across the table and wipes my cheek with her narrow brown hand. "Yes," she says, in very slow, halting German. "But now I find you, Kasia. Now I find you."

I hear a sniff and look up. Marta's mother is crying into a tissue.

"Inge – or rather, Kasia," she says after a moment. "Do your parents – your other parents – know the whole story? About you being stolen?"

I feel cold fingers wrapping around my heart.

"They say they didn't know," I say. "They couldn't have children so they adopted me. They took me from one of the Lebensborn homes in Steinhöring but they've told me they knew nothing of how I got to Germany from Poland."

There's a silence. Deep down I still don't know whether my parents are telling me the whole truth. Another thought has just occurred to me.

"*Matka*," I say, the word still feeling new and strange on my tongue. "Do you have any other children?"

Her face lights up again. "Yes," she says. "You have – how you say? Boy?"

"Brother," says Marta's mother. "You have a brother, Kasia."

I break into a smile. I've always hated being an only child. And now it turns out that I'm not.

"What's his name?" I say.

"Jakub," says Kristina, understanding at once. "He is eighteen years."

So she had him before I was taken. But try as I might, I can't remember him at all.

"And my father?" I say. "Who is he? And where is he now?"

It is as if a cloud passes in front of my mother's eyes. She shakes her head, unable to speak for a moment.

"He is gone," she says eventually, turning my hand over and gazing into my palm. She says something else in Polish.

"He was taken by bad men during the war," says Marta's mother. "He was a farmer. I'm so sorry, Kasia."

"Oh," I say, my heart sinking. I had not expected this. Then I remember all the stories I have heard about what happened to agricultural workers in rural Poland during the Second World War. Many of them were shot and killed by Hitler's men so that Hitler might claim their land for his own. I guess that this was the fate of my birth father.

"So I come to find you," she says, her voice still tripping over the unfamiliar words. "You come home to Poland with me."

I withdraw my hand at this. I look over at Marta's mother and she sees my panic and comes to the rescue.

"Kristina," she says. "You need to give Inge – Kasia – some time. Slow down." She accompanies these words with an exaggerated gesture, pressing down the air around her, to illustrate what she's trying to say.

"I think I should go home," I say. "I mean, my other home. I've been out a long time and they will be worried."

In fact I don't much care how long I've been out, but I've suddenly realized how much the twelve years I've had with my adoptive parents outweigh the few moments of conversation I've had with Kristina. I still feel distanced from Mama and Papa, but right now, I want the familiarity of the home where I've lived with them for so many years.

"Do you want me to drive you?" says Marta's mother. She looks as if she's aged during the last half-hour. Her face is strained and I notice that her hands are shaking.

"No, thank you," I say. I've already got up and headed towards the door. Kristina remains sitting at the kitchen table. She looks quite lost. She stares at me in silence, her eyes pained and pleading all at once.

"I will come back and see you," I say. "I promise. This is just moving a bit fast for me."

I leave Marta's mother trying to explain what I've just said and I run down the corridor and out into the fresh air.

I double over on the immaculate front lawn and vomit until there's nothing left in my stomach except muscle ache.

Chapter Twenty-five

WHEN I GET HOME I'M so tired and shivery that I have no defences up; no energy to lie or pretend or put on a smile. So as soon as I get through the front door and Mama comes towards me with the usual concerned look on her face, I say, "I've been to see my birth mother. She's working at the house of a girl in my class. She wants me to go back to Poland with her but I haven't decided anything yet. So that's what's happened."

I walk past Mama so I don't see her expression. I go into the kitchen and drink two glasses of water to try to stop the sour ache in my guts. Then I go upstairs and lie face down on my bed until the churning inside my stomach calms down and I don't feel as if I'm going to be sick again.

Then I sit up and brush my hair. I go into my

bathroom and scrub the bad taste out of my mouth with toothpaste.

"I'm going out!" I call, but Mama is too quick for me. She's already by the front door, blocking my way.

"Inge," she says, looking straight into my face. "Don't go out. I'm begging you."

This is unlike Mama. I stop on the stairs. Mama has never begged for anything.

"Why?" I say.

Mama crosses her arms so that she's hugging her own elbows. "I don't expect it," she says in a voice which is unusually soft and flat. "But I would like it. You are my daughter, Inge."

"Kasia," I say. "Please call me by the name I was born with."

Mama shakes her head. "I cannot," she says. "I named you Inge and I love it still. I can't call you anything else, I'm afraid."

"Well," I say. "I don't respond to that name any longer. Your choice."

"That's just it," says Mama. "I feel pushed into a corner with this. It's like all the years of looking after you and making sure you have been safe count for nothing. And there's nothing I can do to make you see how much we've always cared for you."

I look at Mama more closely. Her face is paler than usual and I can see that she has been crying. Despite everything, something in my heart gives a little twang of sympathy and regret. But another part of me wants to punish her for lying to me for so long, so I say, "I might even want to go to Poland." My voice sounds hard and strange. I'm not at all sure that I *do* want to go to Poland, but I know that's what Kristina wants.

"If you do, I will worry about you every single minute that you are there," says Mama. "I won't sleep a wink."

"I know," is all I say.

Then I leave, although Mama's vulnerability touches me more than I'd care to admit.

I need to be with Stefan and Wilf and get their advice.

We're sitting in Stefan's battered leather armchairs in front of the empty fireplace. Wilf is making me coffee in the tiny kitchen and slicing up a gingerbread which he tells me he made the day before. There is golden syrup brushed over the top and the warm, spicy smell of the cake is making my gutted stomach feel better even before I've eaten it.

Stefan shakes his head when I tell him what Kristina has suggested.

"It will be very difficult for you, Inge," says Stefan. "You will be leaving two parents who love you very much. You will be leaving your safe and comfortable home. The journey itself will be long and tiring. You will need papers. You've presumably only got papers under your adopted name, but you will need them with your birth name on. Getting out of Germany will be difficult. The train journeys will be long and you may be stopped at the border. And then there's the whole psychological effect of going to a strange country with a woman you hardly know."

"She is my *mother*," I say in a small protest, but I know exactly what Stefan is saying, and that he is right. I hardly know her. I don't know what she likes to eat. I don't know what makes her laugh or cry. I don't know what her parents were like, or anything much about her other child, my brother. I don't even know how old she is or where she was born.

But maybe I should get to know all those things. Because until I do, I can't really make any major decisions about my life.

I accept a slice of gingerbread with a sigh. I feel exhausted.

"What do you think I should do?" I say to Wilf. "Should I go to Poland? See where I was born? Meet my brother?"

Wilf has sat down on the floor at my feet. He has been very quiet since I arrived in the apartment.

"I think you should do what feels right in your heart," says Wilf.

That's a typical Wilf answer. But this time, it doesn't help me at all. My heart feels confused. I truly don't know what I want to do.

"What would you do if you were me?" I press. "Would you go?"

Wilf sighs and rests his forehead on my knees for a moment.

"I don't know," he says. "It is difficult for me to imagine trying to choose between two mothers."

"I'm sorry," I say.

"Me too," says Wilf. He puts his head back on my knee and I play with his hair for a moment. Stefan goes into the kitchen and the dusk begins to fall outside, but Wilf stays where he is and I sit fiddling with his hair, lost in thought.

A clatter from the kitchen breaks the spell and Wilf sits up, looking ruffled and sleepy.

"Inge," he says. "You will promise me something, right?"

"Of course," I say. "Anything." And I mean that. I'd do anything in the world for Wilf and for his father too.

"Come back," says Wilf. "If you do decide to go to

Poland, come back afterwards, okay?"

I am shocked to see that there are tears in his eyes.

"I haven't said I'm going yet," I say. "So you don't need to worry about anything for the moment."

But I can see that Wilf *is* worried. He unfurls himself from his chair and puts on his brown cord jacket. I say goodbye to Stefan and he gives me a warm hug. Wilf takes Stefan's car keys and we go down the stairs in silence to where the old car is parked outside.

We don't talk a lot on the way home. I'm worn out with the emotion of the afternoon and all the conflicting thoughts doing battle inside my head, and Wilf is still thinking about the prospect of me going to Poland, or that's what I'm guessing from the silence.

He drops me off in the close. I look at the lights blazing from Mama and Papa's designer house and for the first time, I feel a real pang of fear.

"I don't know where home is," I say to Wilf.

He comes round to let me out of the passenger side and as I get up, he enfolds me in a warm hug.

"Here," he says. "Here is where home is."

For a moment it reassures me as I breathe in the smell of his jacket. But my life is destined to be complicated now. I know that, even though I don't want to dwell on it.

So I leave the sanctity of Wilf's warm embrace and

cross over to our house as his car drives off in the opposite direction.

I'm so tired and fraught that I have no emotional energy left to pretend or even speak. I brush past Mama as she comes out the house to speak to me, barging my way into the house and not looking back.

"Don't start," I say, speaking with a lack of respect that I have rarely dared show Mama.

I push past her into the kitchen just as she reaches out and grabs onto the banisters for support. I don't look at her face, but I can imagine her shocked expression.

"Inge, we'll wait to hear what your father has to say about all this," she says, in a voice which I can tell she is struggling to keep calm.

"He's not my father," I call over my shoulder from the kitchen. "Not really."

I'm shocked at my own callousness, but I'm fed up with dishonesty and I don't seem to have a lot of control over what comes out of my mouth at the moment. I feel that I've lost patience with everything and everyone except Wilf.

I try to spend the rest of the evening up in my bedroom, but Mama's not having it. She comes in and propels me out of the room and down the stairs into the dining room, where Papa is sitting with an expression very unlike his usual gentle one.

"Inge," he says, gesturing at me to sit down opposite. "This has to stop. You are destroying your mother."

"Not my mother," I say, on autopilot. It seems that, however many times I say this, nobody is going to fully accept it, so I guess I'll just keep on saying it until they do.

"That Polish woman is desperate and deranged," says Papa. "If she'd truly wanted you back, why has it taken her twelve years to come here, hmm? Have you ever thought of that?"

"She did not know where to look until she saw an article in the paper about the work of the Red Cross," I say. "And then you hid her letters. That is why."

The determined look on Papa's face fades to a deflated one. He shakes his head and picks up his newspaper, but I can tell by the way he's holding it that he isn't taking in a single word.

Mama dumps a ladleful of brown stew onto my plate. It is suggested they have waited for me to come home before serving. Sauce splashes over the white tablecloth and splatters the side of her wine glass, but she doesn't seem to notice. Mama never usually allows a speck of dirt to remain anywhere for longer than two seconds so I know she must be feeling really distressed.

"Cabbage?" she says, spooning a mess of greenery onto my plate with a shaking hand. "Gravy?"

I look at the jug full of brown lumps and shake my head. Papa also declines the offer.

Mama sits down and starts to scoop up food with her fork. She eats without looking at either of us. The atmosphere in here is even thicker than the gravy.

In the end she puts her fork down again and pushes the plate away.

"You have even killed my appetite, Inge," she says. "That is quite something."

"Kasia," I say. "My name is Kasia. And you know that, so I wish you'd stop pretending otherwise."

Mama glares at me. For the first time I see very little love in her eyes.

"We took you in and gave you a home," she says. "For twelve years. We brought you here to be our daughter and we gave you a new name to start your new life with. What sort of life would you have had stuck in a tiny village in Poland with a woman who was living in poverty, huh? No piano lessons, no schooling, no cakes or treats or visits to the cinema. What could she have ever given you that we haven't? Answer me that."

I have never seen Mama shake with anger and hurt in this way and underneath my resolve is starting to crumble. But I make myself stay calm.

"Love," I say. "The love of a birth mother."

Mama is not having that.

"No," she says. "Wrong. I gave you that a hundred times over. I have loved you and still love you for every second of every minute of every day and so does Papa. Don't you dare suggest that we have not given you love."

Papa gets up and goes out of the room, holding his hand across his eyes so that I can't see the emotion. Another piece of me cracks. I hate to see Papa cry.

"Well then," I say. "The truth. That is one thing she would have given me that you haven't. And you can't deny that, can you?"

Mama gets up and bangs all the plates into an untidy pile.

"The truth will not feed you, Inge," she says. "The truth will not put a roof over your head and give you a safe and comfortable place to live. You want to go and see how this woman lives in a tiny backwater in Poland? You go and see then. And good luck to you, Inge, because you're not going to like it."

She leaves the room.

I sit at the table, quite alone apart from Papa's newspaper and the worn-down stump of a white candle. I fiddle about with the wax, breaking off bits with my finger and thumb and crumbling them onto the table. My mind is a whirling mass of thoughts. Mama's outburst was hard to hear, but it's lodged somewhere in my brain and is trying to get me to listen.

I know that much of what she just said is true. How do I know what it's going to be like if I go to Poland – that's if I ever get there, what with the border crossing and the lack of identity papers to contend with? Who is going to pay for it? Is the fact that my Polish mother gave birth to me sixteen years ago enough to equal the sort of love and stability that Mama and Papa have given me for most of my life? And then there's the fact that she still speaks very little German. If I try to imagine her and me on a long journey together, I feel a bit sick. What will we talk about? How will she know if I'm feeling ill, as Mama does just by glancing at me? Will I feel safe, like I do when Papa tucks his arm through mine and walks through the city with me? And there's Wilf. How on earth will I cope without Wilf's gentle, warming presence in my life? He doesn't want me to go. But I know he will support me in whatever I choose to do.

That's love, I realize. That's what true love is. And if Mama and Papa can't support me to do this thing, which is so important in my life right now, then maybe their love is not true after all.

I get up and go outside into the front garden to get some fresh air. I sit down on the path amidst the carnations and the dahlias and pluck the grass between my fingers, and after a while I feel calm and resolved and slightly surer of the way ahead, even though it is full of uncertainty.

If I don't go, I will always wonder. Always. So there's my answer.

I know what I need to do.

I'm going to travel back to Poland.

Chapter Twenty-six

I HAD THOUGHT THAT THINGS couldn't get much worse. But when I arrive at school the next day, there's something in the air.

I walk through the gates and I swear that some of the other pupils are huddling together in small groups and talking about me. At first I think that I'm just imagining things. My brain is tired from trying to make sense of everything and I've not slept at all.

So at first I just ignore everybody. But that becomes difficult when I walk past a group of girls from my class and one of them, Eva Krall, turns and spits on the ground in front of me, stopping me dead.

"Dirty Polack," she says, in a voice laden with scorn.

I'm so shocked that for a moment I think I must have

misheard her. Eva's always been quite nice to me in the past. Then I look at the scorn in her clear blue eyes as she looks me up and down.

Another girl comes and stands in front of me.

"Poles are the lowest of the low," she hisses at me. "Scum. No wonder Hitler wanted to get rid of your kind."

I feel dizzy. I look around and pray that Wilf might somehow materialize and rescue me, but he's nowhere to be seen and the grounds are swarming with pupils.

I feel a rising sense of anger. Marta. She couldn't keep quiet even for a day. She had to blab to her friends. I picture her on the telephone, delivering the juicy pieces of gossip with relish. I resolve to beg our teachers to let me sit as far away from her as possible. Then, with another stab of pain, I realize that nobody is going to want to sit next to me now.

Marta is not in school today, though. The fact that she isn't there makes me nervous. What's going on in her household? Has Kristina said something? Or caused something to happen?

I watch the clock all day at school. This of course means that it doesn't move. My lessons drag on and although I copy down passages from the blackboard into the neatly covered exercise book in front of me, I don't recall a word of what I've written. Nobody speaks to me in class at all, although one or two girls whisper about me behind their hands.

I feel very small and alone in school, for the first time ever. I see Wilf at lunchtime, but not for long, as he is heading to chess club. I have just enough time to tell him what happened outside school and he flushes with anger and tells me to come and find him if it happens again.

And so I make a decision.

I will go back to Marta's house – I want to see Kristina.

I still feel nervous walking up the crunching shingle on Marta's drive, past the two large, glossy cars with their sleek interiors of chrome and leather.

I ring the bell and through the frosted glass see the jagged outline of somebody. It's impossible to see who. I straighten my hair and clear my throat, in case it's Kristina.

But it's not. It's Marta's mother. She looks tired, and she's wearing a white apron over her flowered dress. She's not as immaculate as I remember her. Her hair is escaping its bun today and locks of it hang around her face. She hasn't got her bright lipstick on and her face looks suddenly older.

"Oh, Inge," she says. "Kasia. Sorry."

I smile at her for that. At least one person is trying to make the effort to call me by my real name.

"Come in," she says. "Your mother is about to finish for the day, so it's good timing. I also have some cherry cake which needs eating."

I follow her into the large, airy kitchen with the glass roof. There's a warm smell of baking and the cake sits on a white plate in pride of place in the middle of the kitchen table.

There's no sign of anybody else.

Marta's mother fills a white china teapot, gets two smaller plates out of a glass-fronted cupboard and puts them on the table.

A piece of yellow sponge studded with purple-black cherries is slid in front of me. I take a bite. The cherries are soaked in something pungent and slightly alcoholic, and the sponge is fresh and soft.

"Nice," I say, through a thick mouthful. I wash this down with the tea. Marta's mother smiles at me. Her face looks decades younger when she does this.

"I made it this morning," she says. "Baking calms my mind."

I smile back. A lot of barriers have come down between us and I feel as if I'm in the company of an ally.

"What are you going to do?" she says. "About Poland, I mean. Are you going to attempt it?"

I finish my cake and wipe my mouth on the white linen serviette that she's passed me.

"I think so. I want to ask my mother about it," I say.

Marta's mother sighs.

"It won't be easy," she says. "Even if you get onto a train, you will have to cross the border and be checked nearly every step of the way. You'll need ID papers under your real name."

I nod. "I know," I say. "I know it's going to be hard."

Marta's mother pours more tea into my cup. "If you really are serious about this," she says, "I may be able to help you. I'm not promising anything."

I put my cup down at this. My heart gives a little skip.

"How?" I say. "How could you help?"

Marta's mother glances up at the large black-and-white clock on the wall over the fridge. "In about an hour, my husband will be home," she says. "He works in the Foreign Office. So if anybody knows how easy or difficult it's going to be for you to travel to Poland, he will. I will have a word with him for you, Kasia."

I feel my eyes prickling with tears again. This kind woman has come like the answer to a prayer. And more than that, I realize that I am not alone. I have Wilf,

213

and Stefan, and now I have Marta's mother on my side as well.

"He must be pretty important," I say, glancing around at the kitchen with its expensive furnishing and gadgets.

Marta's mother smiles, although her smile is tinged with something else I can't quite work out. Regret, possibly. A secret yearning for something or someone not around any longer.

"Yes," she says. "We have a nice lifestyle. I suppose you could say that I am a lucky woman. Although I will be losing the best cleaner I ever had, thanks to you. I now know full well that she only took the job here to be close to you."

She gets up and calls Kristina's name.

Kristina comes softly into the room and her face lights up into a smile.

Just before Marta's mother leaves the room, I reach out and give her a hug. After a moment, she hugs me back. She smells of soft perfume and starch. It's a comforting combination.

"I'll do what I can," she says. "Now, you take as long as you want with Kristina. In fact, why don't we arrange for you to come here twice a week and catch up? If you'd both like that?"

She repeats the same thing in Polish for the benefit

of Kristina. We look at one another and then both nod, a little shy.

"Thank you," I say to Mrs Schmidt. "You have been so kind and you didn't have to be."

A wealth of emotions pass over Mrs Schmidt's elegant face.

"Oh yes," she says. "Yes I did."

And with that, she leaves us to it.

Kristina sits at the kitchen table with me.

I reach out and touch her hand, shy, and she gives me her joyous smile.

"I have something to tell you," I say. I hope she understands this. She nods and waits, so I decide that she does.

"I want to come home," I say. "To Poland." And as I say it, I know it is true.

Kristina puts her hand over her mouth for a moment. She is unable to speak and there are tears in her grey eyes, but she nods and smiles and pats my hand.

"Good," she whispers in the end. "Good."

We spend an hour in that vast kitchen.

With the aid of pencil, paper and much patience, I have taught her some German words and she has shown me how to write and pronounce Polish ones. I realize when her face lights up into a smile that Kristina is younger than I thought. I can see that hard work and sorrow have made her skin lined and her eyes tired, but when she smiles I can see how she must have looked as a very young woman after she gave birth to me.

Towards the end of my visit, Kristina sketches her Chodecz house on a piece of paper and pushes it in front of me.

I give a little gasp.

It is the house I saw in my dreams. There are the two long, low front windows and the boarding on the front of the building. There is the chimney, belching smoke. And in the background, she has sketched the outline of farms and fields, just as I saw them in my dream.

"I have seen this house," I say, but Kristina does not understand. So I point at the house and mime myself going to sleep as if I am dreaming and then she gets it.

"You know?" she says in her broken German. "You see?"

"Yes," I whisper. I am on the edge of tears. The feeling from the dream hovers in the air in front of me, trying to drag me into fear.

Kristina reaches out and wipes away my tears with the back of her thin hand.

I let her. And for the first time, I feel a grain of comfort.

So I leave, trying to keep a note of hope inside my heart.

What I don't expect the next evening is the knock on the door.

For a moment I think it must be Kristina, come to discuss plans to take me back to Poland.

Mama obviously thinks something similar, because she goes to look out of the front window.

"A man and a woman," she says. "I don't know who they are."

Papa gets up at that and joins her at the window.

"We'd better find out what they want," he says with a sigh. Papa does not like to be dragged away from the dinner table before he's finished either his food or his newspaper. We're all still trying to cling on to some semblance of routine, although it's hanging by a thread and could collapse at any minute.

I hear Mama open the front door and a vague murmuring of adult voices floats through to where I'm sitting.

"You'd better come in," I hear Papa say.

He comes back into the dining room, removing his spectacles and smoothing down his hair.

Behind him are Marta's mother and a man who I realize must be her husband.

"Oh," I say, standing up. "What are you doing here?"

Marta's mother comes over and gives me a kiss on the cheek. I see Mama's expression of surprise.

"Kasia," she says. Mama looks even more surprised at that, and her faint smile of welcome has faded away as if it never existed. "We thought it best, given the enormity of what you're hoping to do, that we discussed it with your parents. You are, after all, technically still a child."

I sigh. I don't feel like a child. I haven't felt like a child since the day I went to Steinhöring with Wilf.

Papa leads our guests through into the large stark living room on the opposite side of the corridor. Mama gestures to Marta's mother and her husband to sit in the comfortable white leather armchairs which make a circle in the middle of the room. There's an awkward silence while Papa goes over to the oak sideboard and removes a bottle of brandy. Our guests accept a small glass each, and then we're all sitting in a circle staring at one another, Marta's mother crossing and uncrossing her legs in their black stockings and Papa trying not to look and Mama noticing and glowering at him. It feels like some sort of bizarre dream.

And I'm sitting there with all four of them looking at

me with varying degrees of concern. I wish that Wilf was here. Because despite the looks of concern, I don't feel much warmth coming from anybody, except maybe a little from Marta's mother.

"Your daughter wishes to travel to Poland," says Marta's father, making me jump a little. He's a small man, with a black moustache and glasses and very little hair left on his head, unlike Papa. I have a hard job placing him together with Marta's mother, who is taller than he is and glamorous, even with the shadows underneath her eyes.

Mama and Papa exchange glances.

"Yes," says Mama. "We are trying to advise her against it."

I give a small snort at that. Mama ignores me.

"I'm sorry," she is saying. "But what exactly have you two got to do with any of this? You say you're the parents of a school friend?"

Marta's father sighs and removes his glasses.

"We're employing Kasia's birth mother as our cleaner," he says. "And as a member of staff at the Foreign Office, I have been looking into the complications of travel from Munich to Poland and how Kasia might attempt it, should she decide to travel."

Mama gives me a look. I find it hard to read. It's a

mixture of frustration, impatience and something else – resignation, perhaps. She knows better than most people that when I set my mind to something, I generally achieve it.

"And?" she says. "What have you found out?"

"Anneli," says Papa. "That's a little rude. These people are trying to help by coming here." He pours more brandy into our guests' glasses by way of trying to compensate for Mama's brusqueness.

Mama ignores him and continues to stare at Marta's father.

"Well," he says, "I have tried my best. But it is a complicated business. I can't pull any strings, I'm afraid. The journey would be difficult at the best of times. I'm sorry, Kasia. I wanted to tell you in person."

I give him a weak smile for using that name. "Thanks anyway," I say. "Now what do I do?" I picture Kristina's narrow, anxious face.

"Well," says Mama, "that's that. If you can't get there, Inge, you can't go."

I note the pointed use of my old name but I'm not going to rise to it today.

"There must be some way," I say. "I haven't given up yet. There's got to be a way."

Even as I say this, I realize that I sound desperate.

How can I, a sixteen-year-old girl, cross countries and borders with no proper identity papers?

Papa has been very quiet. He's sitting with his hands clasped across his knees, leaning forwards and just looking into my face.

"Would it truly make you happy to go, pumpkin?" he says. The use of my old nickname sends a pain through my heart.

"I think so," I say. "I'm scared as well. But I want to see where I come from. Where I was born. Do you understand that?"

Marta's mother and father have faded out of the room. I hear Mama bid them a polite, cold goodbye and then she comes back in and stands with her hands on her hips.

"You're causing no end of trouble, Inge," she says. "Making those good people come out at night. You should stop this nonsense right now and let us all get on with our lives."

But Papa has stood up too. He comes over to my chair, crouches down so that he is on a level with my face, and takes my hands in his.

"Our daughter is unhappy, Anneli," he says. "And we should try to help her."

This is such a surprise that I feel the familiar tears, never far from the surface, threatening to spill over again.

Mama sits down with a sigh on the edge of a chair, and buries her face in her hands for a moment.

"What are you suggesting, Josef?" she says. "And why do I feel that I'm not going to like it?"

"Probably because you're not," says Papa, with a smile at me. I smile back. I forgot that Papa and I used to be kindred spirits, before all this started.

"Spit it out," says Mama. "I've still got to do the dishes."

"Well," says Papa. "We…I still have some clout in the military. So I'm going to get in touch with a couple of old friends and see what I can do."

Mama gets up and leaves the room, just as I knew she would.

Papa traces one of the tears as it falls down my cheek.

"She'll come round," he says. "It's hard for her, Inge. To know that the woman who gave birth to you is here, is taking you back to your original home. She is hurting."

I nod. I know, really. I can see it, although Mama hides hurt behind a barrage of sharp words and abrupt gestures. But I'm too far gone with this now to want to change my mind.

"Thank you, Papa," I whisper.

"I can't promise, Inge," he says. "But I will try."

He kisses my cheek. Then he goes back across the hall to his newspaper.

From the main bedroom above where I'm sitting, I hear Mama trying to hide the sound of her tears.

Chapter Twenty-seven

FOR THREE MORE DAYS, WE carry on some semblance of normal family life.

The house doesn't feel like home any longer. It feels like somewhere I'm lodging while I'm waiting for the next part of my life to start.

I don't push Papa for information. The day after Marta's parents came to visit, he got up earlier than usual, put on the smart black hat that he keeps for funerals or business meetings, straightened his tie in the hall mirror and left just after dawn, leaving a whiff of hair oil and aftershave hanging behind. Mama did not kiss him goodbye that morning, as she usually does. She stayed at the back of the house with the kitchen door wide open, throwing bundles of laundry into the machine and then pegging them out on the line in the backyard. She hadn't spoken to me since I got up that morning. All she did was put a bowl of porridge in front of me, poured some juice into a glass so violently that most of it ended up on the table and then took the bowl and glass away again when I'd finished.

I left for school without either of us having said a word.

My days at school are filled with almost as much tension and uncertainty as my days at home are. The only relief I get from any of it is seeing Wilf and so I do this as often as I can.

I'd like to go and visit Kristina again. But I want to go with good news and at the moment I don't have any. I want to tell her that arrangements have now been made for us to travel together back to Poland. But there seems to be so much standing in the way of that happening. I can't rely on Papa to make everything right. But I know he will do his best for me. And that makes me feel better, but guilty. He's always been a wonderful father to me and our relationship has been about as close as a daughter and father's could be.

Then I think about the father I never knew. The Polish

one, who was murdered during the war. I wonder if any photograph of him exists, or if my birth parents were too poor to have ever had their picture taken. Because my parents have kept the truth from me all these years, I've never known of the existence of this other father. My birth father. And I feel angry inside whenever I think of this.

There's so much I want to ask. So much I need to know. But there's the language barrier to start with, and the journey, and the fact that I will be a foreigner in a strange place many, many kilometres away from home.

You were taken many kilometres from your home, says a voice inside me. *So you are only going back where you belong.*

That doesn't make me feel any better. I wish I had a good friend at school to confide in, other than Wilf. There's nobody I feel I can open my heart to since Marta blabbed and now half the class view me as a dirty Polack. Hiding wouldn't help anything though. I know I need to face things. There's been enough hiding and secrecy in my life up until this point. It feels a relief to decide that there won't be any more.

I go home from school with a heavy heart. I don't look forward to getting there any longer, but it's where I live, so I have to go there. Mama barely speaks to me, and although I see that she is hurt, I'm starting to detach from her, viewing her as a stranger might.

I see a square-jawed woman with shoulder-length blonde hair in waves and cool blue eyes, which often now have a look of fear in them. I know she wants to reach out to me, but my rejection is stopping her. I realize with a shock that Mama is actually starting to be afraid of me. The loving, laughing girl that she brought up for twelve years is becoming a stranger. And there's nothing I can do to stop this now. It's as if I need to disconnect in order to prepare for my new life.

My relationship with Papa is a little better, although he too does not speak to me as much as he used to. But his eyes still twinkle at me from time to time, even though there is an air of sadness hovering over him also.

"How is your schoolwork coming along?" he says to me each day before supper. "Anything nice planned with friends for the weekend?"

I can see that it is costing him an effort to ask these questions, because he knows that my mind is very far away from life here in Munich. I know that he is suffering underneath.

I know that I am going to miss him terribly when I go away.

* * *

I've just come home from seeing Wilf and Stefan. I've had a chicken stew cooked for me and we've played games on the floor of their living room, and for one afternoon I've felt like a normal person. I haven't cared much whether I'm Inge or Kasia. I've just felt like me.

As I walk up the path to my front door, Mama surprises me by coming out of the house. She's clutching her handbag and putting her keys inside it as if she's leaving in a hurry.

"Oh," she says, seeing me. "I'm going to the shops. Won't be long."

I know that this is a lie, because she always takes the same shopping basket to the shops and she's not holding it. I can see that she's been crying because her eyes have shrunk and are red-rimmed. I can only guess that she and Papa have had a row.

Then my heart gives a little jolt. I push past her and go into the house, where Papa is standing in the kitchen, leaning against the sink with his arms folded and a stunned expression on his face.

"Oh, there you are," he says. "Inge, I have some news for you."

I know, straight away. Behind him on the kitchen table I see a selection of small pieces of paper. I go over and start to examine them.

"You've got your identity papers," explains Papa, although he does not need to, because I am holding the white document in my hand and on the front of it there is a photograph of me which I sat for just over a week ago and there, underneath the photograph, my name is given as *Kasia Pietrowski* and my birthplace as *Chodecz, Poland*. Kristina's name is listed and so is my real birth date, which is the same as the one I've always known.

I get a thrill of something sour inside me. This is becoming real. It is really happening. I can feel that something has been set in motion now and that I will be unable to resist the pull of it, however scared I might be.

There is also a series of printed train tickets.

"Some for you, some for your mother," says Papa. With a jolt, I realize that he's referring to Kristina. It's the first time he's ever referred to her in this way. "Your friend's mother told me that Kristina had no return tickets. So I got them for you both to Poland. Then you will come back alone."

I put the documents back on the table and come over to where Papa, my papa, is standing by the sink. I hug him tight. We haven't done this for ages, and at first he stands stiff, not hugging back. But then he relents.

"I'm not happy about any of it, pumpkin. And you'll have to miss a week of schooling too, just before the summer holidays start," he says. "Mama's heart is breaking.

And so is mine, although perhaps I cope a little better. But we feel as if our little family is falling apart."

I keep my head against the warm green wool of Papa's sleeveless jumper so that he does not see my tears. But he feels them, because I'm shuddering.

"Inge," he says. "I'm sorry. I can't use your other name. It's just not what we know you as here. Forgive me. But I am worried about your journey still. You will be stopped many times and checked. It will be a long and very tedious trip for you and you will be with somebody who does not speak much German. I am wondering if I should come with you?"

I pull back so that I can look at Papa's face.

"How would that work?" I say. "You couldn't really expect to stay in that house. Besides which, I'm not sure that Kristina would like it."

Papa sighs. "I'm worried about your safety," he says. "That's what fathers do. And I'm still the only one you've got, remember?"

I nod. Papa kisses the top of my head and wipes his own eyes.

"Please try and make up with Mama," he says. "She's not angry, even though she might look it. She's just frightened of losing you for good. Please don't leave things on bad terms."

I get myself a glass of water. I feel dried out with weariness and strong emotion.

"I'll try," I say. "But I don't think it's going to be very easy."

Papa gives me his warm smile. "Good girl, Inge," he says. He leaves me looking at the documents and goes outside to his shed.

At break time the next day I run to find Wilf.

He's in the common room. I don't take any notice of the fact that he's talking to a group of his friends. I break through them and grab him by the arm.

"I'm going," I say, breathless. "I'm going to Poland. Papa got me the travel documents."

Wilf's friends melt away into the background. I wait for his reaction. I know that he always takes his time responding. At last he takes my hand in his own thin one and gives me a gentle smile which is tinged with something else.

"I'm pleased for you," he says. "Really I am. A bit worried about not being there to look out for you though. Are you sure you don't want me to try to come with you?"

For a moment I am tempted. The thought of having Wilf by my side in a foreign country makes it a far more

231

attractive idea. But I also know that I have to make this journey with Kristina and spend some time with the two of us alone together, so I kiss him on the cheek, shake my head very slightly and then leave the common room to head back to lessons.

I think about Wilf for most of the afternoon during double maths. I can't imagine my life without him in it. I would sooner cut off my own arm. He is what makes me smile when I open my eyes in the morning and makes me feel comforted when I think of him last thing at night. I carry him around in my heart all the time and I know that he does the same with me. He and I are so bound up in one another, so used to speaking to each other every day and sharing every thought that passes through our heads, that if I think about him not being there, for any reason at all, I feel dizzy and as if somebody has replaced the ground with quicksand. I know that he'll still be in my head and my heart all the time, even if I go to Poland, but the thought of his physical presence not being there is causing me to wake in the night catching my breath in a panic.

Wilf. His broad shoulders and thin arms and wrists. His soft, blue-grey eyes, with their concerned expression.

The depth of his hugs. Wilf, despite his slender build, hugs like nobody I've ever met before. His hugs come from somewhere deep inside and they seem to speak volumes to me without him even uttering a word. The first time he hugged me like that, the traffic noise around us fell quiet, even though we were in a park by a main road. I felt shaken, like something of great importance had passed between us and that I would never be the same again. And I was right, because although I'm sixteen and Mama says I'm far too young to be in love, I loved Wilf from that first hug and I still love him now.

I'm so frightened to leave his warmth behind in Germany and travel all that way with a woman who is still a stranger to me. But I must.

After school I run all the way to Marta's house. In my brown leather satchel I have a wallet containing the papers and tickets that I'll need to get to Poland and I've been checking and rechecking that they are in there all day – so much so that at one point I dropped them on the ground and almost risked them being blown away by a strong gust of summer wind.

Marta's mother opens the door and smiles when she sees me standing there.

"Kasia," she says. I love her for using that name. "Come in. Your mother is here too."

I get that shot of nervous adrenalin at the mention of Kristina. This is all still so sharp and new and strange. But even now, there's the beginning of some sort of bond between us. Sometimes I swear I can feel her thinking about me, even though I'm at home alone in my bedroom. I just get a sensation. And I've started to think that the nightmares appeared as a message, in a way, showing me what happened when I was younger, so I trust these sorts of instincts and feelings.

I get the documents out of my bag, and spread them on the table for Marta's mother to look at.

"My," she says. "Your papa must have been pretty high up in the army to arrange all this for you. What exactly did he do?"

I shrug. "I'm not too sure," I say. "Some sort of general, I guess. I know he was in charge of a lot of men. But all my life he's been an accountant, so it's difficult for me to imagine what he did in the war. Where's Kristina?" I ask. "I'm dying to show her the papers. Or at least...I think I am. I'm a bit nervous."

"Of course you're nervous," she says. "You're about to change your entire life, Kasia. That would make anyone nervous."

Suddenly I realize we're not alone. A small presence in the doorway makes me look around. There stands Kristina, in her grey dress and cracked leather shoes, but today her head is bare and, with a jolt, I see that her hair is much the same honey-colour as my own. There's plenty of it too. She has it tied back in a bun, but if she were to take it down, it would probably fall beyond her waist.

"Ah, Kristina," says Marta's mother. "Come and join us. Kasia has something to show you."

Kristina's eyes have lit up at the sight of me. She comes over, a little hesitant. She sits down at the table in the chair next to me and reaches out, putting her narrow hand on my wrist. We look right into one another's eyes and this time I force myself not to look away out of shyness, or fear, or embarrassment, or all the other sensations I've had on previous occasions. This time I look right into the grey-flecked eyes of my mother and I see generations of my Polish family stretching back inside those eyes and they are all holding out their arms to me.

"I can come home with you," I say, pulling the documents across the table towards her. "I have the papers."

She has no idea what I am saying, but she smiles at my Polish name on the papers and then looks at me, her eyes bright with hope.

"And tickets for you too," I say, pushing the printed squares under her nose.

She picks them up and looks at me again. "For me?" she says. "How?"

I decide that I need to be honest. "My Papa," I say. Her face looks confused for a moment at that, and I know why. She is thinking of the Papa I will never know. Then she remembers, and nods.

"He is a good man," she says. "Good man. I will thank him, yes?"

I consider this for a moment. I can't really imagine Papa inviting her into our house. Mama would probably explode.

"I don't think you need to," I say, but she doesn't understand this, so in the end I give my softest smile and say "no."

She nods. I think she understands what I am trying to say.

"Home," she says again. She is holding my wrist very tightly now, so tight it makes me wince. "Yes," I say. "Home. I am coming home for one whole month."

Kristina reaches out and touches my cheek with her hand. No more words are necessary.

When Marta's mother comes back five minutes later, she finds us sharing a piece of cake and grinning at one another, shy but happy.

* * *

Things at home are not so good.

Mama is trying to distance herself from me a little. Now that they know I'm going, there's nothing they can do or say to stop me, although Papa is still worried about it.

The journey is booked for the beginning of July. I am to stay out there until the second week of August and can then come home during the summer holidays. Papa has given me return train tickets but I will have to make the journey back alone as Kristina will be staying in Poland. I can't yet think about how it will feel to leave her behind.

Papa has already warned me that life in Communist Poland is harsh, and many years behind our comfortable life in Munich. He has told me to expect to be shocked, to not be able to wash or eat well and for people not to be welcoming, given that I am German so far as they are concerned.

His warnings have dulled my excitement a little. There are times, in the dead of night, when I wake up in a sweat and think that I don't want to go at all.

Chapter Twenty-eight

EVERYTHING SEEMS TO SLOW DOWN for that final week.

I see Wilf whenever I can at school and we talk on the telephone every evening and he is gentle and kind, asking if there is anything that he can buy me to take to Poland and of course I say no, because Wilf has no money at all. And in his voice I hear a tremor and I know that he will miss me as much as I miss him and possibly more, because I will have the distraction of a new country and a new life but he will just see my empty chair in his apartment.

I ask Mama if I can take some time off school to sort out my packing and get my head around the enormity of what I'm actually about to do, as we're heading for the school holidays anyway, but she tells me that I should not let anything interfere with my education.

I want to go and spend some more time with Kristina before we go back to Poland together. When I tell my parents where I am going, they want to come with me.

"We should meet her properly," says Papa. Mama doesn't say anything, but she gives a curt nod. I know that this meeting would be difficult for her though and that there would be tension. Which is why, in the end, I tell them not to come – and they agree, although I can see it is not what they want.

The thought of going on a train with Kristina for over a day is making me nervous. We will have to somehow communicate with one another on that journey and during my stay. So I arrange with Marta's mother to call by and pick Kristina up on one of the days that she cleans for the Schmidts. I suggest that we walk around the Old Town together and try to bond a little more.

The day does not start well. When I arrive at Marta's house, I find the family in a state of stress because their cook has walked out without giving any notice, so instead of preparing for a day out with me, Kristina is standing at the sink, peeling potatoes, and there's a smell of meat roasting in the oven.

"Oh," she says, seeing me come into the kitchen dressed in my neat blue flowered dress and gym shoes.

She looks down at her apron and the traces of flour on the sleeves of that long grey dress. "I cannot go."

Marta's mother goes over to the sink and unties Kristina's apron from the back.

"Of course you can go," she says. "We'll manage. It's not like I've never cooked before."

"We're all going to die," Marta says darkly. She's sitting at the kitchen table, chewing on the end of a pencil. I recognize the book she's supposedly studying from as our algebra textbook and I feel a pang of anxiety. My schoolwork is sliding backwards at an alarming rate and I know that I won't be winning any prizes this term.

"Less of that, thank you," says Marta's mother. "Show some respect, please."

Marta rolls her eyes at me and returns to her homework.

Kristina thanks Marta's mother, brushes the flour from her sleeves and ties her grey headscarf on, ready for us to leave. It feels strange to be going with her on an outing.

We walk in warm sunshine for a little while in silence and I try to think of things to say, but the language barrier still makes it difficult to chat.

In the end we stop walking and sit at a cafe in the Marienplatz area of town. I've got the money that Mama gives me every weekend for helping out around the house, so I buy us a couple of cups of coffee and two pieces of chocolate torte. Kristina's eyes light up at the richness of the cake. I watch as she forks the first mouthful, raises it reverently towards her lips and then closes her eyes to enjoy the texture of the chocolate ganache.

After the waiter has cleared our plates away, we sit with our faces turned up to the sun and for a moment there is another silence which is more comfortable. But Kristina has remembered something. With a little cry of triumph, she produces a tiny black-and-white photograph from the pocket of her dress and passes it over to me.

"I forgot to show," she says, shyly.

The photograph shows half of what I recognize to be the house from my dream. In front of the boarding underneath the window stands a small boy of about seven or eight years old, staring with a solemn expression at the camera.

"Jakub," says Kristina, looking at me. "You remember?"

I stare again, but I can't remember a thing of this little boy who I now know to be my brother, and the photograph is too small for me to pick up on the closer details of his face, so I can't see if there is any resemblance to me or even to Kristina.

But she's still smiling at me, waiting for my reaction. So I smile back and nod, even though I know I'm not telling the truth.

"Soon, you will see," she says, tucking the photograph away again and draining the dregs from her coffee cup. I get a nervous feeling in my stomach at the "soon". I have a brother who I've no memory of. I've lived all my life as an only child. I'm worried that I won't be able to communicate properly with my brother if he only speaks Polish. I'm worried that after all these years he might resent not being the only child any longer and somehow take it out on me. I guess my main worry is that it will be like visiting a stranger and that we will never become friends.

We walk around the Old Town together, stopping to look in shop windows and to watch some of the street entertainment. Kristina jumps a little when our famous clock begins to strike, but then she smiles and looks up at it with fascination. I picture the tiny house she's lived in all her life and realize that everything in Munich must look colourful and large and opulent by comparison, even though she has told me that here in Munich, she is lodging in two small rooms in a run-down apartment block.

I look at Kristina's face in profile. I see that it is full of hope.

I try to push away any thoughts of home. Today is about me getting to know Kristina better and by the time I walk her back to Marta's mother's house we are both tired but happy. I don't know her well enough to kiss her yet, but she does hold my hand for a moment and give me her shy, anxious smile, and that's enough for me right now.

When I get home, Mama is still distancing herself from me. I know why she's doing it but that doesn't make it any easier to deal with. Despite everything, I want her advice on what to take with me to Poland. I don't know whether to take warm clothes or lighter, summer ones. I need to buy new things and she usually comes with me when I shop for clothes. I can't really ask Papa and now it doesn't feel right for me to ask Mama. So I sift through my clothes, trying to sort them out as best I can and squashing as much as possible into my small brown suitcase.

Mama cooks, cleans and shops but we barely exchange a sentence now.

Papa tries to make amends for her coldness, but even he is struggling.

"I don't know how to make this any better," he says to me one evening in a low voice.

"I don't think you can, Papa," I say. He holds my hand and we sit in silence.

* * *

As the day of my departure approaches, a strange thing happens.

The dreams return. Maybe it's because I've been picturing the tiny house in Chodecz so much this week, or maybe my mind is trying to prepare me for what lies ahead, but I wake up in a hot sweat of panic from the first one. The details in the dream are almost exactly the same. I see my mother run out into the street, and I feel the rattle of the cartwheels beneath me as the horses drag me away from the tiny village. I see the fields and hills and the square red tower of our church. I feel that same sense of rising panic and disbelief, but this time as I open my mouth and try to call to my mother, I am thinking in my head, *The Nazis are taking me, Matka! The Nazis are taking me.* And it seems very important that I should tell her this, or how else will she know? How will she find me?

I wake up fighting for breath and boiling hot. I fling off the eiderdown and lie there, trying to calm myself. It's not easy. For the first time, it truly hits home that I will soon be walking into the place I was stolen from all those years ago. I don't know how it is going to make me feel. The memories at the Lebensborn home in Steinhöring were hazy, but even they provoked a strong sense of fear and made me unsettled.

For one short, miserable moment I want Mama. Not

my birth mother. Mama. I want her to come into my room and sit on the edge of my bed and sing to me as she did when I was a little girl. I want to tell her that I feel afraid and sick when I think of the future and for her to soothe away my worries and make them all better. I want her to bring me up a hot chocolate like she does when I'm ill or tired, and to watch her draw the thick red curtains across my windows and tuck in the quilt around me, click on the bedside lamp, kiss my forehead and then gently shut my door.

Tears spring to my eyes. I'm so tired. I've been waking up in the middle of the night for several days now and once I'm awake, I can't seem to get back to sleep again. It feels as if everything is slipping and fading away and I'm being hurtled towards something that I have very little control over.

I miss Wilf already and I've not even gone yet.

I reach under my pillow and pull out the photograph of Wilf that I keep there all the time. It's my favourite picture of him. He's wearing an old sweater of Stefan's, which is too big, and baggy trousers, and he's bending down in the courtyard of the apartment building, tinkering with the wheel of his rusty bike. The photograph reeks of Wilf – of his attention to detail, of the care he takes when doing anything and everything. He looks capable and approachable all at once. Just after I took that photograph last winter, he came over to me in that oversized sweater and put his arms around me and we had one of those hugs which you never want to get out of because it makes you feel so good, so safe and protected from the rest of the world.

I need to hold onto that memory. When Wilf holds me like that, I feel absolutely myself. It doesn't matter whether I'm Inge, or Kasia. It's about how I feel inside.

The morning of my departure for Poland dawns cold and grey, almost as if the weather is trying to prepare me for what lies ahead. It doesn't resemble a summer's day at all.

Papa will be taking me to the Marienplatz station this morning. I will be meeting Kristina there. Marta's mother has offered to bring her to meet me.

Because I desperately want to say goodbye to Wilf and Stefan in person, they have agreed to meet me early in town under the clock. I will have to find a reason to leave the house this morning for twenty minutes.

Papa is up before me, laying the table for breakfast and cutting slices of brown bread. This is so unusual that I stop dead in the kitchen doorway.

"Where's Mama?" I say. She's usually down here doing the breakfast while Papa gets shaved and dressed.

Papa comes over and plants a kiss on the top of my head. He looks pale, as if he hasn't had much sleep, and he hasn't shaved yet or combed his hair.

"She'll be down," is all he says, but his voice is subdued. "It's a big day for her too, Inge. I know you don't want to think about that, but you should do."

I sit at the kitchen table and pick at the bread and butter in front of me. I thought that Mama was going to make more of an effort. But she seems to have changed her mind again. I have no appetite. I keep glancing at my suitcase, which is just visible in the hallway. Everything seems to have slowed down and taken on huge significance. I am buttering bread with a knife which seems larger, colder and more shiny than usual. The butter takes an age to spread across the bread. Even the lifting of the bread to my lips seems slow, considered, laden with significance this morning. I realize it's because it is the last time I will do these everyday, mundane things here in this house for quite some time. I find it hard to swallow. This is all so real. I really am leaving my home without Mama and Papa for the first time in my life, and travelling the long distance to a foreign country with a woman I hardly yet know.

"Papa," I say, dizzy with fear. "Papa, I don't have to go, do I?"

Papa wipes his hands on a tea towel and comes to sit down with me. He takes my hands in his and looks straight into my eyes. "Of course you don't," he says. "Nobody is forcing you to go. You wanted to, remember?"

I nod. I can't speak for fear and tears. I almost wish that Papa was not being so nice and caring. It would make it easier for me to leave if he would wash his hands of me, ignore me or say something cutting and cruel. But Papa has never been like that. He is a good, kind, honest man. That thought brings me comfort. I know that, I think, and I will always know it.

"Will Mama come down to see me off later?" I say. "I want to say goodbye to her properly."

Papa kisses the knuckles of my right hand and gestures at me to eat something. "Of course," he says. "We will not see you for a whole six weeks and we will miss you so much. Of course she will come and say goodbye."

I manage to swallow a few mouthfuls of the bread, washed down with strong, sugary tea. Then Papa checks his pocket watch and asks to be given the little wallet in which I've put my papers and tickets. He checks through them very carefully. He has spent some time explaining to me which ones are which and where on the journey I will need to produce the various identity cards.

"All there," he says, tucking the wallet back into the

zip pocket of my shoulder bag. "We've got about an hour until we need to leave, Inge."

I'm ready with my excuse.

"I want to walk into town," I say. "To say goodbye to everything. I won't be long."

Papa frowns, but then nods. "Alright," he says. "But please don't take long. You mustn't miss that train."

I walk in the drizzle towards the clock where I last sat with Kristina. Because it is still quite early, there are just a few people around and a mass of pigeons peck and waddle around the square.

I only see the tall, lanky figure of my beloved Wilf and Stefan's shorter frame hovering behind.

"Hi," says Wilf, kissing my cheek. He looks stern, unsmiling. He slips a book into my pocket. "For the journey," he says. Then he turns aside and lets Stefan hug me.

"I have brought you some gingerbread, little Inge," says Stefan. His warm eyes are wet. "Look after yourself. We are going to miss you."

I wait for Wilf to say the same, but he's looking down at his feet and then out over the Old Town as if he's got an appointment somewhere else and I'm keeping him.

"Wilf," I say. "I've got to go. Papa is waiting for me."

Stefan retreats tactfully into the background at this point. Wilf steps forwards and puts his hands on my shoulders. "It is only six weeks," he says. "I will write to you. Okay?"

Now my tears are coming. Six weeks seems an eternity in the world that Wilf and I have created together.

"I hope so," I say. "That will keep me going. And if I don't like it, I'm coming straight back."

Wilf gives a little smile at that. He wraps his scarf around my neck. "Keep it," he whispers.

Then the clock strikes nine and the spell is broken.

"Bye," I whisper, reaching up to kiss his cheek. I smile at Stefan through my tears.

Then I walk away from those two dear people without looking back.

When I get to the house Papa is upstairs and Mama is nowhere to be seen. I go into the dining room and look at the polished oak table where I've spent nearly every evening with my parents. Then I wander into the study and try not to look at the drawer in Mama's desk where my quest started. It seems an age since Wilf picked the lock and I took out the pile of letters in their cream-coloured envelopes. I consider the painting of Hitler which still hangs on the wall in here. "I was stolen because of you," I whisper.

I go into the living room and trace my shoe along the shiny edges of the parquet floor where I used to run as a little girl.

"Time, Inge," says Papa, materializing at my side. I can tell from his voice that he is trying to be practical and firm and cheery, only he doesn't sound any of those things and I can hear the tremor in his words.

I don't go upstairs to my bedroom. I don't want to admit to myself that I won't be sleeping in it tonight, that in all probability I will be sleeping on a train and then arriving in the dead of night in some unfamiliar village in the middle of an unfamiliar country where nobody speaks my language.

So I pick up the brown leather suitcase with the label bearing my Polish name, and I walk out of the front door of the house without looking back.

I have given up on Mama coming. I heard her moving around upstairs earlier, but she never came down for breakfast. I don't comment on this, but inside I feel gutted, flat and miserable as if I've been hit in the face by yet another unpleasant truth. Mama maybe doesn't love me enough to come and wish me well.

"I'm sorry, Inge," says Papa. "I think she's just finding

this a bit too painful. I know that she wishes you well, pumpkin. I really do."

But I just can't believe that.

And then, as Papa is starting up the ignition, the front door of the house opens and Mama flies down the path in her pink dressing gown, her hair unkempt and her face unwashed and contorting with something that looks like grief or pain, and she bangs on the window of the passenger seat where I'm sitting. I get out of the car and she enfolds me in the tightest hug she's given me in a very long time, and when we finish hugging she holds me at arm's length and looks straight into my eyes and she says: "I know you don't want to hear this any longer, Inge. But I am your mother and I love you. I'll always love you and be here for you. Don't you forget that."

She shoves a small bag into my hand. Inside are some sandwiches wrapped in waxed paper, two apples, two thick pieces of her home-made fruit cake and a bottle of lemonade. There is also a small flask of coffee.

"For you and for her," she says. "You will both be hungry on that journey."

It is the first time Mama has made reference to Kristina in a long time. My eyes fill with tears. I reach out and give her a kiss on the cheek.

"Can't you come to the station?" I whisper. "Please?"

But Mama is already retreating towards the house. I realize that there is now a gulf between us that may never be healed. I know that some of this damage has been done by me insisting on travelling to Poland and I feel a flash of guilt at the way my stubbornness has crashed into our little family unit and ripped it apart. But I'm still angry enough about my letters being hidden for all those years to make me want to continue on my journey and find things out for myself.

So we leave her standing in the close, hugging her elbows and gazing after the car.

Papa and I don't speak much on the journey.

I look out at the familiar streets of the city and everything seems to have slowed down again. I see the expressions on the faces of the people as they look in shop windows or sit at cafes. I watch the trams rattle by; hear that particular whine of their electric rails. I note the rigid tails of dogs as they trot alongside their owners. I see the road which leads to my school, and for a moment I picture the classroom with my empty seat in it.

I glance at my bag on my lap. I'm trying to convince myself that all this is real, that I'm really going. I think back to this time last year, when I was oblivious to everything. I got up, ate breakfast, went to school, visited Wilf and came home again. That was my life.

But this is my new life. About to start here, now, today, at this train station.

My stomach feels sour with nerves. Papa is pulling into a parking space. He switches off the ignition and turns to face me.

"Well, pumpkin," he says. "Let me just savour this last, quiet moment with you. Once we get in there, you'll be on a train and gone before I know it."

He turns back to the steering wheel. I notice he's still gripping it.

People stream out of the station, zigzagging in front of our car, hailing taxi cabs and heading for tram stops. They look as if their journeys are commonplace, but who knows? I will look like that to others. Just a girl and a woman with suitcases, getting on a train together. Who could possibly guess the story beneath the everyday scenario? What would the other passengers say if I told them I was stolen by the Nazis and sent to Germany to be adopted by a childless couple, and now I'm going back to Poland with my birth mother?

I shiver, even though it's not cold in Papa's car.

He reaches out and puts his arm around me, pulls me towards him. "You'll always be my girl," he says. "Always.

And if at any time you run into trouble out there, or you don't like it, you can always come home. You can use your return ticket at any time. Understand?"

I nod. Papa's jumper smells warm and familiar. I ache with homesickness suddenly. And I've not even gone anywhere yet. I still have that image of Mama in my head. Her pale face against the pink of her dressing gown, and the way she hugged herself and became a tiny dot in the rear-view mirror as we drove away from her and my home and former life.

"Come on," says Papa. "Otherwise I'll be tempted to drive you home again."

I smile. "I wouldn't mind if you did," I say in a small voice. But we both know that I'm committed to doing this now. Besides, if I didn't go, I would always wonder what might have happened. What my real brother looks like. What the room I was born in is like. I want to smell the air in that tiny village, look at those hills and go inside the church with the square, red-bricked tower. Most of all I want to stand with my eyes shut in the middle of that street, and I want to connect with the ground and the air and the sky of my birthplace and I want to feel what it is like to be Kasia Pietrowski again.

"I'm ready," I say. Papa gets out, takes my bag and offers me his hand.

The buzz and hum of the station forecourt threatens to overwhelm me for a moment. It's just a sea of people, most of whom seem to be in a haring rush. My bag is jostled and pushed into me as we make our way towards the correct platform. The hiss of steam from a train just coming in makes me jump.

"That's yours," says Papa. "Don't worry, it will sit here for half an hour. Plenty of time."

I'm hanging onto his arm now. The front of the train is black, immense. People are opening the doors and jumping off, slamming them behind them. I glance about in a panic.

"Where are they?" I say to Papa. "If she doesn't come, then I can't get on the train, can I?"

There's a tap on my left shoulder. I turn round. Marta's mother is standing there. And next to her is my birth mother. Kristina.

Her face breaks into an uncertain smile when she sees me. I can tell that she's as nervous as I am.

"I don't think any of us slept well last night," says Marta's mother. She does look somewhat stretched beneath the eyes. I notice that Kristina's hand, when she reaches out to put it on my arm, is trembling a little.

We stand on the platform making awkward conversation for ten minutes, with Kristina straining to understand anything we're saying. All the time I'm standing there, smiling and trying to act as if this is a perfectly normal occasion, a sense of panic is rising up inside me.

"Inge, you will be fine," says Papa in my ear.

I ignore the use of my old name. I'm starting to realize that Papa won't be able to call me anything else. And that, actually, I don't mind any more.

"Thank you, Papa," I say. "And thank you for all this. For arranging it and for understanding."

Papa kisses the top of my head, clears his throat and wanders over to a newspaper stand. I'm not fooled by that for a second. I have tears in my eyes too.

"You'd better board," says Marta's mother. "You don't want to miss this train."

I look at Kristina. She looks back at me, her eyes bright and nervous. Then she extends her hand towards me. Papa comes back and joins us. After a second's hesitation, I take her hand and we walk towards the train.

Matka.

Papa puts my bag onto the train and then comes back to me. He enfolds me in a tight hug.

"Take care of yourself, pumpkin," he says. "Already I am looking forward to you coming back."

I'm crying for real now. The world outside has vanished. It's just me and Papa standing still in the middle of this busy railway platform.

"Tell Mama…" I begin. Then I have to compose myself in order to be able to speak clearly. "Tell Mama I love her," I say. "Please."

Papa laughs. "She knows that," he says. "She's always known it. But of course I will."

Kristina is saying goodbye to Marta's mother. "Thank you," she says, in halting German with that strong Polish accent. "Thank you."

Marta's mother kisses Kristina on the cheek. "Go well," she says. "I am so glad that you and Kasia found one another and that it happened in my house. Fortune was smiling on us that day, no?"

I can see that Kristina doesn't understand the last part of that sentence at all, but she is smiling at Marta's mother and nodding as if she does. They grip hands for a moment. Then Papa helps Kristina onto the steep step of the train and into our carriage.

The guard is nearby with a whistle in his mouth and a flag in his hand, and the great train is hissing and bellowing black smoke. The clock overhead shows two minutes until departure.

I linger, holding back. I'm cowering in Papa's arms now. Kristina is giving me anxious glances.

The guard looks up at the clock and prepares to blow

his whistle. He gestures for me to get onto the train.

"Inge," Papa says. "Get on the train with Kristina. Now."

"I've changed my mind," I say in a panic. But Kristina has already boarded the train and is holding her hand down to me and Papa is pushing me up seconds after the whistle has blown. He slams the door just as the great bulk of the train begins to heave its way painfully along the tracks.

I hang out of the window. There, on the platform, growing smaller, is my darling papa, waving his hat and blowing his nose on a large white handkerchief.

I look for as long as I can, until he becomes a small dark dot.

Then I turn around. Kristina is sitting by the window, looking down at her lap. Suddenly I have a strong recollection of the time I was pulled away from her. When, screaming with fear and pain, I was dragged off the street by the woman in brown and watched my mother becoming a tiny dot at the end of a village street.

Am I always destined to be leaving? When will I arrive at a place to truly call home?

Chapter Twenty-nine

FOR THE FIRST HOUR OF that journey, we don't speak a single word.

The train rattles through the outskirts of Munich and then beyond, into wide open countryside.

I sit next to the woman who gave birth to me sixteen years ago and I feel shy and strange and tired from the early start this morning. I'm in her care now. That is a strange thought to come to terms with. No longer can I rely on Mama or Papa to see me through the next six weeks. This woman is going to feed me and put a roof over my head.

We sit side by side in a silence which is companionable but laced with a sharp, new edge. I already miss Wilf. The lack of his voice hangs in the air and torments me. I will have to hear his voice in my head, I decide. And I will have to try to remember the feel of his arms around me. Tucked into a pocket on the side of my brown leather bag I have some of the notes and letters that he's written me over the last three years. A surprising number, given that we see each other so often. But Wilf is a keen lover of words, and he likes to express himself. So I have the precious letters with me. I don't think I can get them out now, however. Kristina would think that I'm being rude if I do that, and I don't want to get off on the wrong foot.

So I ferret about in the bag Mama handed me just as I left, and I pull out the small red flask which is usually kept under the kitchen sink. Even that association causes a twinge of pain in my stomach. I open it and pour a stream of hot coffee into the white plastic cup. I offer it to Kristina and after gesturing to me that no, she couldn't possibly take the first drink, she sees my face and relents and nods her thanks at me. I watch as she cups her hands around the plastic and sips at the good coffee. Mama has used some of her precious stash of proper ground beans. The earthy smell of the coffee reminds me of Sunday mornings at home, when she would sometimes allow us a cup each of the proper brew.

"Is good," says Kristina, closing her eyes and inhaling the steam from the cup. She passes it back to me and I sip it, nodding in agreement. "Your mama is kind woman," she says, causing me to look at her in surprise. She hardly knows Mama. And I did not think she would ever say a good word about the woman who adopted me from the Nazis.

"Yes," I say, after a moment. "She is kind in her heart. Not always on the outside, you know?"

I'm not sure Kristina understands this. But she smiles and pats my hand as if she does.

We lapse back into silence as the first ticket inspector approaches the narrow length of the train. We sit back and gaze out of the window as West Germany turns to East Germany and the landscape becomes less familiar and less green.

I start to recover a little from the painful departure at the station. Kristina turns and gives me a shy smile once in a while and I can see that she is making an effort, so I smile back. In my head, I try to make sense of my thoughts. I realize that many people would consider me to be lucky. I have the love and support of two mothers. Two good mothers who want to protect and take care of me. I should feel like the luckiest girl in the world. But of course I don't. Because there is conflict involved. Conflict and being stretched in two directions and pain all round. Two mothers, so very different in nearly every way. The only thing they have in common is me.

Later on, Kristina goes to sleep, leaning against the window as the train rocks and jolts. We have left Germany and crossed the border after the guards have stamped us out. I no longer recognize anything outside the window. I wait until she's been asleep for a few minutes, and then I pull out one of Wilf's precious letters and I read it for comfort, trying to hold the page still enough. It is more of a note, this one, sent about a year ago, after we went for a long walk around the Old Town.

Dearest Inge, it says. *It was so good seeing you today that I can't wait until next time we meet before telling you that. I felt so proud walking into the Old Town with you at my side. It makes me feel good when other people look at me and see that I have a girlfriend like you. It fills me with a sort of old-fashioned pride. It makes me want to look out for you, to love and protect you always. Thank you for being you, Inge. You fill my life with warmth and colour and joy. Yours, Wilf x*

I love Wilf's way of writing. He writes like I do. Sometimes it's like reading my own words coming back at me. We have the same sense of humour, the same likes and dislikes and the same romantic nature. Reading his words is such a comfort, albeit with pain attached this time, that I find myself smiling and even laughing at one point as I read a couple of other letters. I lose track of the fields and buildings passing by outside and just envelop myself entirely in Wilf. By the time I've finished reading all of the letters, Kristina has woken up with a start, looking at me with fright in her eyes.

"It's okay," I say. "I'm still here."

She smiles, reassured.

I look at my watch. It's getting on for lunchtime. I pick up Mama's bag again and pull out the sandwiches filled with potted meat and tomato. I pass one to Kristina and after a quick inspection of the insides, she eats it with approval. I eat half a sandwich, and a small piece of Mama's fruit cake. The familiar smell and taste of the food produces more pangs of homesickness, but I know I need to eat and I've no idea what Polish cuisine is going to be like, so I reach for another sandwich and give the last one to Kristina. Then I use Papa's pocketknife to slice up a red apple and we finish our train meal with that and a swig of Mama's sharp, sweet lemonade.

My tickets are checked by an unsmiling guard in a black uniform. He gives me a searching look and spends even longer looking at Kristina's tickets, but in the end he nods and hands the tickets back to us. My heart pounds hard with the relief.

After that we settle back into our seats and fall silent again. Papa has told me that at just past two we will need to get off this train and get onto another, so I keep an eye on my watch and I try to note the names of the stations as we pull into them, but they are no longer in German and even though Papa has written the name down clearly, I struggle to match his spidery black scrawl to any of the names we are going past. So I show Papa's note to Kristina and she nods. The name is Polish, of course.

We pull into a small station with only a handful of people waiting on the platform and she points at Papa's writing and nods again, so we grab our bags and tumble out onto the platform. The air is sharper, colder here. There are guards and officials in uniform hanging around next to the train, talking and giving all the passengers suspicious looks. I shiver in my thin jacket.

I'm tired, too. The lack of sleep and the long journey so far are starting to make me feel numb and stiff. But I know we've got several hours still ahead of us and that it will be nightfall by the time we finally reach our destination. So I eat another slice of fruit cake on the platform, breaking it into pieces and offering some to Kristina, and she eats it while looking up and down the track for our next train, tapping her foot on the platform and pulling her scarf more securely around her head to stop the chill of the wind.

Just when I think I can't stand waiting here much longer, another train moves into view, a small black dot at the end of the track. When this one pulls in I feel less sure about getting on it. The trains in Germany were sturdy and clean, despite the billowing smoke. This one is lugging a line of carriages which have clearly seen better days. They are ancient, with wooden sides full of splits and gaps and the windows are smeared with mud and dirt, as if the train has come right through the middle of farmland, which it probably has if Papa is to be believed. He told me that the scenery as we begin to pass through rural Poland will be very different to what I am used to. The train doesn't inspire much faith.

But I step up onto it, turning to offer Kristina my hand. She bounds up, surprisingly nimble. We take our seats inside the dirty, run-down carriage. There's a stench of something unpleasant in here. Kristina doesn't seem to notice it, but I pull Wilf's scarf up over my mouth and breathe in the familiar smell of him.

This train is not a smooth ride. It grinds its way slowly past fields and farms. I see men working in those fields, and heavy horses pulling tractors across the farmland. I notice something else. The further we get into Poland, the more relaxed Kristina becomes. She is looking out of the window now, smiling to herself. Her increasing calm is in direct proportion to my growing nervousness. She senses this, and pats my hand from time to time.

"It is all good," she says in her strange broken German. "You will see. You will see home."

Home.

The word floats in and out of my head for the rest of the journey.

We travel on for what seems an endless amount of time. The tension between us has disappeared now. We're sitting in silence, each lost in our own thoughts, but from time to time, Kristina looks into my face as if to check that I'm alright, and then nods to herself and returns her gaze to the darkening landscape outside. We have passed through kilometres of farmland. Some of the farmers glance up when the train rattles through. We are in the middle of what looks like nowhere as the sun begins to go down. I sense a change in Kristina. She is sitting upright and is searching for something outside. A station pulls into view. *Włocławek*. Kristina grabs my hand and hustles me off the train.

We stand, dazed, in the fading light for a moment, our bags at our feet, and then she gestures for me to leave the station via a tiny exit at the very back. There is what looks like some sort of bus station outside. Kristina looks at her pocket watch and then squints at the timetable; checks her watch again.

"One hour," she says. "One hour."

She sits down, so I realize that we've got one hour to wait here and I sit down next to her with a sigh. I'm so tired. The past few weeks have caught up with me. All the tension and uncertainty have gone, replaced with this bone-aching tiredness. I'm still apprehensive, but at last I don't have to worry about upsetting Mama and Papa and creeping around their house, trying not to cause further argument.

"I can just be me, now," I say, more to myself than anybody else. Kristina looks puzzled, so I smile and shake my head. "It doesn't matter," I say. I offer her the remaining fragments of fruit cake from Mama's parcel and we share it in silence, watching the dusk turn to darkness. Finally a brown, single-decker bus heaves into view, and I get on, squinting in the lights of the vehicle. Kristina says something I don't understand and flashes two of Papa's tickets at the driver. She seems to know him, for they have an animated conversation in Polish and he shoots me the occasional look and raises his eyebrows at her, until the other passengers begin to complain from the back of the bus. He throws a comment over his shoulder which sounds like an insult, crunches the gears of his bus and lurches back onto the road without bothering to check if there's any other traffic.

Kristina grabs me just in time as the bus swerves.

"Drivers all crazy," she says in her halting German. "Poland."

I'm starting to realize that there are a lot of things I'm going to have to get used to. Even the air smells different here – rich, earthy, with a sharp note on the top which I can't identify. I reckon it may be a vegetable smell, from the farms all around us. My stomach makes a little noise of protest. The cake and sandwiches have only just taken the edge off my appetite. Normally by now at home I'd have eaten one of Mama's meat stews. I never went to bed hungry.

The bus grinds on for nearly an hour. I lay my head against the window and drift off from time to time, jerking back into consciousness with a stiff neck. Kristina observes me with her bright eyes, but says nothing.

At last the driver shouts "Chodecz!" and even though his pronunciation of the word is very different to the way I've been trying to say it at home, I recognize what he's saying and my heart leaps into my mouth.

Home.

We are deposited at the side of a dusty road just outside the village. I can see the cluster of houses ahead, some with dim lights showing in the windows, and I know that I am about to walk into the setting of the nightmare

I've been having for so many years. I feel dreamlike even though I am awake. I pinch my arm just to make sure it's real and the skin dimples and aches, so I pick up my bag and we begin to walk towards the village.

I sniff the air. Beets, potatoes, manure. The farmland smell is stronger here. I can see the dark outlines of fields and, beyond, what looks like a dense stretch of forest set against the curves and dips of distant hills.

We trudge together into the heart of the village.

I'm standing in the street from my dreams. At last, I'm actually here. We are passing by that striking, red-towered church, and beyond it I sense the shifting mass of a dark expanse of water and realize that there's some sort of lake in this little village too.

Kristina is walking ahead of me now, with purpose. She has shaken off the tiredness of the journey. We pass down the village street which I already feel I know so well, but other details come into view. The wooden slats on the tiny houses. Front doors with chipped paint. The sounds of voices speaking in unfamiliar accents from behind windows, some with dirty net curtains, others without. Dogs, chained up in front gardens or backyards, barking at something or nothing as we pass by. The hum of machinery coming from a factory where smoke belches out from a tall chimney.

Gone is the comfortable, affluent feel of the close in Munich. I can almost sniff poverty in the air here, a feeling of unsettledness, of difficulty. But also there's a sense of community, enhanced by the church at one end of the street and a tiny, low white school building at the other. I pick up on the closeness of all these people without really knowing how or why. I just do.

Kristina has stopped. We are outside a small grey house with two main windows fronting the street and a chimney billowing a dark stream of smoke into the night.

She turns to me and I see the whites of her eyes shine in the darkness.

"Home," is all she says, but I already know.

She opens the door by pushing it inwards. There's no sign of a key. A dog inside begins to bark. A smell of woodsmoke engulfs me as I enter, and something else. A cooking smell, which I can't place. It could not be more different from the smells of polish and beeswax and washing powder which fill our house in Munich.

I note the paint flaking off the walls, the religious paintings hanging at odd angles over a tiny black crucifix.

"Come," says Kristina.

She bustles into a kitchen at the back of the house and I follow, feeling exhausted and shy in equal measures. I am very aware that I am a stranger in a stranger's house. I feel a sudden pang of longing for my crisp white bed at home. But this is my new home, at least for the next six weeks. So I follow her into the kitchen and put my bag down in the corner with a sigh.

Kristina removes her headscarf. Underneath, her hair is wound into a tight bun. She gestures at me to remove my jacket, and I do, because although outside the night was cool, in here there is warmth coming from a small fireplace stacked with logs.

"Jakub!" Kristina calls, in a sharp proprietary tone which shocks me. I've never heard her raise her voice before. But now she is not in Marta's house being a cleaner, but back on her own territory. As she moves around the kitchen, opening cupboards and laying the small table in the middle, I realize that the only reason she has been shy and quiet is because she has been out of her own environment for too long. It is I who am shy and quiet now, because I am very much out of mine.

"Sit," she says, pointing at the table. A plain white plate is put in front of me, and a hunk of brown bread follows it. There is a pot boiling on the hob and when she lifts the lid, a rich, savoury smell follows. My stomach growls. A piece of dark purple sausage is put on the plate next to the bread, and a bowl of hot broth follows.

"Jakub!" Kristina calls again. She shakes her head with impatience.

"He is lazy," she says. But somebody has obviously made the soup, and I'm guessing that, as Kristina's husband is gone, her son, my long-lost brother, must not be as lazy as all that.

I begin to dip a spoon into my bowl. It tastes of beetroot and potato and some herb which I can't identify, and it is thick and filling. I have never had soup like this before. I glance around the kitchen as I eat. I notice that, despite the lack of furnishings and the very basic table, chairs and stove, it is very clean.

"Ah," says Kristina.

I stop looking around and follow her glance towards the doorway.

A boy is standing there. A fair-haired young man some two years older than me, wearing a white shirt, shorts and red braces, standing in scuffed black leather lace-up shoes that remind me of Kristina's. His eyes are fixed upon my face. He is not smiling.

"Kasia," says Kristina. "Jakub. He is brother."

I smile, despite myself. I stand up and approach Jakub, holding out my hand. He surveys it for a second and then takes it in his for one brief second before dropping it again.

"Jakub," says Kristina. She says something to him in Polish and I can make out the word for "sister".

Jakub gives me a brief nod. He goes to the table, takes a piece of bread, bites off a chunk of sausage and then leaves the room.

Kristina sighs. She is playing around with her soup. "He is, how you say? Surprise?" she says.

"Shocked," I say. "He looks shocked."

I don't tell her that I am feeling shocked as well. And hurt at Jakub's aloof reaction. I had thought that he'd be excited to see me, or at least ask me some questions. But instead, we hear him clumping around overhead and then coming down the stairs again to slam the front door behind him.

Kristina puts more bread on my plate and passes me a bowl of thick butter.

"We must sleep," she says. "No?"

"Yes," I say. My eyes are drooping and it's all too much to take in. I feel deflated since the arrival and departure of Jakub. He's my brother. Shouldn't we both feel something more than edginess and awkwardness? I was ripped out of his life twelve years ago and now I'm back. Something more momentous should have just happened between us, rather than a bored-looking eighteen-year-old boy staring at an exhausted sixteen-year-old girl.

But I'm too tired to dwell on this any longer.

Kristina puts our plates in the white sink beneath the window and takes me up a small winding staircase which comes out on a tiny landing with only two rooms off it. This part of the house seems to be some sort of roof extension to what was originally a one-level building. She opens up the door of one of the rooms and lets me enter.

"Jakub's room," she says. "Yours, now."

"Where will Jakub sleep?" I say, alarmed. No wonder he hasn't given me a good reception.

"He will sleep down the stairs," says Kristina, so I guess she's referring to the tiny front room I passed on my way in.

I look around my new bedroom. It has sloping rafters on either side, one small latched window looking out over the village street, and a wooden dressing table with a bowl upon it. The floor is bare boards and the walls are white and devoid of decoration, but there's another small black cross nailed to the wall over the head of the bed. Marta's mother told me that Kristina and her family were devout Catholics and I'm starting to see evidence of this in every room of the house.

In the centre is a small black iron bed with a green quilt on it.

Kristina puts my bag on the bed and opens it, despite

my murmur of protest. She pulls out all my clothes, admiring the material of some of the expensive dresses and skirts that Mama has bought me over the past year, and hangs them up in the narrow cupboard set into a corner alcove of the room.

I sit on the bed and look around the room.

"Where did I sleep as a little girl?" I say. Kristina shakes her head and I know she doesn't understand, so I point at myself and mime a shorter version, and then I press my hands to my cheek and close my eyes. She understands right away.

"Come," she says. She takes me by the hand, as if I was still four, and leads me across the landing into a room which is a little bigger. This one has a double bed in the centre and I realize with a pang that this must be where she slept with her husband.

Kristina bends down and pulls at something beneath the bed and, to my surprise, another bed slides out, already made up with blankets and a pillow.

"Here," she says. "You sleep here."

I gaze down at the low bed on the floor, and for the briefest second I remember what it felt like to trail my hand over the side in the night and run my fingertips along the cracks in the floorboards while my parents breathed softly in their bed above.

Kristina is smiling at me, watching my face.

"Ah," is all she says, but it's enough. I smile back, and then a wave of total exhaustion washes over me and I stumble back into the other little room, remove my clothes with relief and slide under the clean, smooth sheets of the single bed.

I fall asleep almost straight away. I don't recall Kristina coming in to turn off the light but she must have done, because I wake up in the blackness of the night and I am in total panic.

I lie in bed, trying to calm myself. I can hear strange noises outside: the endless barking of dogs, the arguing of a man and woman somewhere nearby, the hum from the factory which never seems to sleep. Kristina told me earlier in her halting German that it makes coffins.

I toss about, sighing, and some of my noise must have filtered through to Kristina because the door to my room opens and she comes in. She puts the light on and sits on the edge of my bed.

"No sleep?" she says. "Not good."

I give her a weak smile, relieved to be back in the light again.

"I'm okay," I say. "I think. It's just all a bit...new. But old as well. Confusing."

I know that she doesn't quite get what I'm saying,

but she pats my hand anyway. She's wearing a shapeless white nightdress, her feet bare. Her long hair flows loosely around her face, thick and dark blonde in colour, although tinged with those grey streaks I noticed after I'd seen her for the first time. She looks about ten years younger than she does in her work clothes with her hair tied up and I realize with a pang of surprise that Kristina is a beautiful woman, that she must have been desired and loved by her husband, that once she must have been an even more beautiful young woman.

Now that the night has brought down any remaining barriers between us, I also notice the sadness and love in her grey-flecked eyes. I see her looking at me, trying to claw back some of the twelve years she has lost, trying to piece things together, make sense of what happened.

I still can't really believe that I'm here. Only this morning I was sitting up at dawn in my plush bedroom in Munich. And now I am sitting in a tiny attic room in a village in the middle of the Polish countryside, a long-haired woman with a heart-shaped face gazing into my eyes.

"You sleep now," says Kristina, pulling the covers back up to my chin. She leaves the bedside lamp on, guessing correctly how frightened I was in the pitch black. "*Dobranoc.*"

"*Dobranoc*," I say back to her, my tongue falling over the unfamiliar word, which must mean "good night". But somehow it feels good answering her back in her own language.

I turn on my side so that I'm facing the bedside lamp. This time I sleep until morning.

Chapter Thirty

I WAKE TO AN UNFAMILIAR NOISE.

Outside, a chain of heavy farm horses are being led down the middle of the village street, pulling carts laden with vegetables. I watch as women dart out of their houses, hastily pulling on headscarves, many of them barefoot. The horses stop long enough for the women to barter and throw their arms in the air and choose what they want from the carts and then they are led on their way again.

I watch, entranced. All I ever see at home in Munich are the shiny cars of the other residents revving up and driving off towards the city.

There's a great babble of chatter in the air. I'm starting to realize that Polish people are very expressive. I can hear my own birth mother shouting from the downstairs window at a group of women and they come over to her and continue an animated conversation, with her hanging halfway out of the window. I wish I could understand what they were saying. I feel a little afraid about the language barrier and how I'll fit in around here.

I use the bowl of water on the dresser to wash my face and underneath my arms, because I'm guessing that there is no bathroom up here, and then I pull on a clean blue cotton dress and canvas shoes and push my hair back with a blue band. There's no mirror, so I use the window reflection as best as I can. A fair-haired German girl looks back at me.

Jakub, my brother, does not look as fair as me. His skin is darker, as if he's been working out in the fields for a good while, which I'm guessing perhaps he has. I saw him looking at my fair skin and blonde plaits with something bordering upon distaste.

I shiver, and make my bed, plumping up the one single pillow and smoothing the green quilt. Then I creep down the narrow staircase and make my way into the kitchen. It looks different in daylight. I see for the first time the cracks on the cupboard underneath the sink, the faded and uneven grey stone of the floor and the way in which the window doesn't quite sit as it should in the frame.

But the kitchen table is scrubbed until it gleams, and on it is a bowl and a plate, and at the stove, Jakub is frying potatoes and eggs in two separate pans.

I hesitate for a moment. Then I go and sit at the table.

"Good morning," I say, remembering my manners.

He turns around from the stove and gives me a brief glance.

"*Dzien dobry*," he says. I'm hoping that this means "good morning" and not something insulting, but as Kristina comes in with a shy smile and says exactly the same thing to me two minutes later, I'm reassured.

Jakub must be the same age as Wilf, I reckon. Wilf. I get a pang of guilt when it occurs to me that I haven't given him more than a passing thought since I got here. But I think he'd understand that I have a lot of new things to take in just at the moment. I make a mental note to write him a letter later, even though I suspect it will take a long time to reach him.

I thank Jakub as he puts a plate of food in front of me, and two more plates for himself and Kristina. I smile up into the face of my brother, hoping for a smile back. But he avoids my eye.

We eat in silence. Our first breakfast together. Kristina is trying hard to make things normal, offering the odd comment in Polish to her son and then smiling at me apologetically, topping up the strong black coffee in my cup and spooning more egg onto my plate when she realizes that I've got an appetite.

Jakub stares at his plate the whole time he is eating. He shovels in his food as if it were the last crumbs in the world. Then he gulps the entire cup of coffee, wipes his mouth on his arm and scrapes back his chair.

He grabs a cap from a hook by the door, puts it on and leaves. We see him head off down the village street. I'm guessing he must be going to work on the farm. It must have been difficult for Kristina, losing my birth father, her husband, at such a young age. Jakub has had to fill his father's shoes both at home and at work. He must have had to keep everything running while Kristina spent time looking for me in Munich, too.

I finish my breakfast and stretch my arms behind my head. I'm wondering what Kristina has in store for me today, but to my surprise she is passing me my jacket and shoes from where they've spent the night on a kitchen chair.

"Come," she says.

I am led up the village street and past the tiny white school building.

Children are straggling up the street and disappearing through the wooden double-doors. Some of them are young, barely old enough to let go of their mothers' hands. Others are older, like me. I realize that all ages are taught under the one roof, which is not what I am used to in Munich at all.

I am glad that Kristina does not stop with me at this building. I have no desire to go to a school where I do not speak the language and where everybody will stare at me.

Instead I am pulled by the hand around the tiny village of Chodecz, with Kristina knocking on nearly every door in the street, or sometimes just walking straight into people's houses. It seems that nobody locks their front doors here. I think of the security bolts and chains across the front door of our house in Munich and the way the neighbours twitch their curtains and spy upon visitors to the close.

Kristina is welcomed and kissed and hugged and shouted at in loud dramatic voices. Women pinch my cheek and exclaim when Kristina proudly explains that I am her daughter, and although I can't understand the Polish, there's no mistaking the look of pride and warmth in her eyes.

In every house I go into, I am fed. Even though I've just had breakfast, the women in these tiny wooden buildings press bread and cheese and bits of sausage into my hands and pour the endless bowls of black coffee which I'm starting to realize are part of the staple diet in Chodecz. I can see from some of the insides of these houses that nobody has any money at all, but it doesn't stop their generosity with food.

After an hour of being introduced to the villagers, Kristina points at her watch.

"*Obiad*, twelve," she says. She's telling me to be home at midday for my lunch. She kisses my cheek for the first time and I'm surprised to find that I don't mind all that much, even though it feels very different to the firm kiss wreathed in clouds of perfume that Mama used to give me every morning. This kiss is light, as if a moth has landed on my cheek.

Kristina heads back to her house. She has told me that there are jobs to be done and later she too will go out and work on the farm that her husband left behind. Part of me is terrified at being left to my own devices in this unfamiliar place, but another part of me is excited.

I walk down the village street in the direction of the red-towered church at the end. There is a graveyard a little further down, and I stop, dazzled by the difference between this and the stark cemeteries back in Munich. The graves in this place are set within little gardens of their own. There are benches and rockeries and even tiny wooden gates dividing one stone from the next. The gravestones themselves are adorned with flowers and photographs, some of the photos set into the gravestones themselves, others just positioned in frames nearby.

I open the gate of one of the tiny gardens and go in, even though it feels a little bit like trespassing. There's nobody in the cemetery, and I need some peace and quiet to think. I sit on a hard bench and say a silent thank you to the man whose photograph is beaming at me from his gravestone.

From here I get a view across the village to the large lake beyond and the hills behind them. I can see tractors and horses moving slowly like ants across farmland and see the thick plumes of smoke coming up from the coffin factory, which has been in Chodecz for over a hundred years.

The sun is bestowing a little warmth, even though there always seems to be a chill wind underneath. I lift my face up to it, and close my eyes for a moment. It is so quiet. I can only pick up the distant hum of the tractors, the sounds of birds and the heavy clop of horses' hooves as they pass up and down the village street.

I absorb these sounds, trying to link them back to my childhood. My memories are very hazy. I realize that they've probably been wiped out by the following twelve years of being brought up in Munich. I try hard to feel or sense something which comes from my early life, but in the end I give up and just sit in the peace of this colourful graveyard. It occurs to me that, other than Kristina, nobody knows exactly where I am and nobody can contact me. I get a brief flash of fear when I think this, but it's replaced by a surprising sense of pleasure.

Sitting here, near to the place where I was born, I can, for the first time in ages, just be myself. I am not Mama's daughter. I am not a pupil at school, or even Wilf's girlfriend. I'm just myself. I don't need to answer to anybody for the next hour or so and there's something liberating and exhilarating about knowing that.

Lebensborn child.

I open my eyes.

The spell is broken. I get up and wander down to the lake at the very end of the village. It's a vast, calm expanse of water, with nothing floating on it to break the illusion of glass. I can see the church from here and I wonder if Kristina got married to my birth father inside, and if he might be buried in one of those little gardens. I make a mental note to ask her later.

I walk alongside the water for a while. It's cold here again, so I pull down my sleeves and do up the buttons of my cardigan.

The novelty of being on my own has worn off as

quickly as it arrived. I shiver, missing Wilf's warm arms around me and the way his eyes crinkle up at the sides when he smiles down at me.

Absence brings pain, I think to myself. Then I think of how my absence must have brought Kristina over twelve years of pain, true pain. I check my watch, head back to the village street. It is almost twelve.

When I arrive back at the tiny house I find the door open and a rich smell of soup is coming from the kitchen. Kristina is already ladling it out into a cracked white bowl.

Her face softens when she sees me come in. She sits me down at the small wooden table and I eat the rich beet soup that she's made with vegetables from the farm.

"After," she says, pointing at my bowl, "I teach you *polski.*"

I smile. I was hoping that she might do this. I'm picking up the odd word and Papa warned me that it is one of the hardest languages to learn and it had taken him years to understand complete sentences. But I want to try.

When the bowls have been washed up and put away, Kristina wipes the table and brings me a piece of paper and a pen. I know she won't possess anything like Papa's shiny new dictionaries, so I'm guessing she'll write the words down and then we'll work out the translations, and that's exactly what she does.

We start with the basics. She teaches me the Polish word for "father": *ojciec*. I already know the words for "mother" and "brother" so then we move onto words for other things.

She teaches me the word for "house", which is *dom*, and then for "street", *ulica*. I listen to her pronunciation of each word and then try to repeat it back, and she's patient and kind, although occasionally I see her trying to stifle laughter at my worst attempts. By the end of the afternoon I am able, with some faltering, to say an entire sentence:

Nazywam sie Kasia i urodziłam się w Chodecz.

My name is Kasia and I was born in Chodecz.

I'm so pleased at being able to speak a whole sentence that I repeat it to myself under my breath for the rest of the afternoon, because I don't want to forget it.

It feels precious, to speak in my native tongue.

For the first time I am starting to feel like Kasia.

I begin to settle into my new temporary life in Chodecz.

The first few days are spent exploring, mainly on my own. But after that, Kristina takes me to the farm with her in the morning and I help her dig up the beets and potatoes that form the mainstay of our meals. She ties a headscarf similar to her own over my head, to stop me burning in the sun, and finds me a long grey apron to tie over my dress, and heavy boots with laces for my feet. I look at my face glowing in the mirror after my second day spent outside and I see the beginnings of the ruddy complexion that I've seen on the faces of so many Polish children in this village.

The work is exhausting, but somehow satisfying. It stops me missing my other life in Munich and even from missing Wilf too much. I start to adjust, bit by bit, to early dawn starts and late afternoon finishes, and the always-present meals of soup and bread and sausage, and I see a strong and healthy girl in my reflection and I begin to like the person I see looking back at me.

One day Kristina hands me the mixing bowl and the ingredients to make *pierogi*, the soft Polish dumplings that she often serves at the midday meal.

Under her watchful eye I mix flour, salt and eggs into a soft dough and knead it until it becomes stretchy and smooth. Kristina fries onions, the sharp, savoury smell making my stomach growl with hunger, and mixes them with potato and cheese. She lets me roll the dough and shape it into circles using the rim of a cup and then spoons her mixture into the centre of each. We pinch the edges of the *pierogi* together until each one is sealed into a little half-moon, and then drop them into a battered brown saucepan of boiling salt water for a couple of minutes until cooked.

"You are fast," says Kristina, with an approving nod.

I smile. I have spent years helping Mama prepare food back in Munich. I find the act of cooking comforting. It slows down my brain and shifts the focus into my fingers.

We eat the *pierogi* brushed with melted butter and ground salt and they are the most delicious thing I have ever tasted. In the end I gulp them down so fast that we make another batch and eat those as well. All the time Kristina watches me eat, her eyes bright with love and approval.

After that she teaches me a new recipe every day for the midday meal. We make *bigos*, a traditional Polish stew made with cabbage and sausage. We make *gołąbki*, cabbage leaves stuffed with meat and rice. And as a treat one day, Kristina shows me how to make *sernik*, a rich Polish cheesecake quite unlike anything I've ever had before. All the time we cook, we talk in bits of Polish and German.

I'm starting to feel at home.

There's a dance in the school hall. Kristina tells me that I should go to it and meet some of the other children the same age as me. I pull a face. I don't like dancing or being forced to talk to boys, and besides, I hardly know any of the language.

But she insists. So on the Friday night of my first week, I find myself wearing lipstick and with my hair neat and shining down my back, standing at the side of the village hall with my arms folded and wondering how much longer I'll have to stand here feeling like an idiot as everybody else dances past me in couples. There's a group of musicians playing the violin up on a small stage at the front, and the music has a strong folk feel. It is impossible not to tap a foot to the music, but even so I feel out of place and strange and am mentally writing a letter to Wilf in which I tell him how alien all this feels.

Then I feel it.

Breath on the back of my neck.

Slow, deliberate breath with a faint odour of stale soup attached to it.

Something tells me not to turn round.

"German pig," says a voice behind me. "We don't want you in our village or even in our country, German pig."

Whoever it is has a faultless German vocabulary.

Despite my instincts telling me not to, I have to turn round.

Our eyes meet. I jolt with shock.

Jakub.

I had a vision, before I travelled to Poland.

I imagined that my brother would have spent the last twelve years desperate to have me back in his life. I pictured his face, white with shock at the age of six as Kristina had to explain to him that his beloved younger sister had been stolen from the very street they lived on, never to be seen again.

I thought that he must have lived with a black hole of absence in his heart. That he and Kristina would have sat down in the tiny house and looked at my photograph and fretted over where I was and how they could ever find me and get me back.

And of course, that may well have been what happened. But when Kristina told him that I had spent the past twelve years living with a German family, something changed.

I spend the rest of the dance trying to fight back tears. Jakub disappears from the hall, but the evening is ruined for me.

I miss Mama and Papa all of a sudden. So much that it hurts.

I don't want to go back to Kristina's.

But I've got nowhere else to go.

* * *

Back at the house, Kristina is pouring a steaming mass of boiled potatoes into a bowl. She turns around and gives me her worried smile. She's bareheaded again, but her hair is tied back in a long snake down her back and she's wearing a knee-length grey dress.

"Good?" is all she says, but with enough hope to make me realize that I'm going to have to lie.

"Yes," I say, forcing a smile. I sit down at the tiny table. I feel lost and alone and very, very far from home. I miss Wilf so much that it hurts my stomach for a moment. I need his arms around me and his cheek up against mine.

It's late at night, but a bowl of thick beet soup is put in front of me, along with a plate of potatoes and some coarse red sausage. My stomach growls, despite my unhappiness. I know that the beets will have been picked from the farmland just across the road earlier that morning and the potatoes dug up from the adjacent field. There is no butcher's shop as such, but a butcher drives a van through the middle of the village every morning and sells his meat products from door to door.

I take a bite of the sausage. It is rich and salty and bloody, but I like it. The potatoes are soft and fragrant and the beet soup sharp and sweet at the same time. I wonder as I'm eating it if the reason that I like it so much is because somewhere inside me, I remember eating it when I was a little girl.

The food distracts me for a moment and then I remember.

"Where is Jakub?" I say. Even saying his name makes me feel nervous.

Kristina smiles. "He no come home," she says, choosing her words with care. "He is with friends." She gestures with her head towards the houses on the opposite side of the street and I guess that Jakub has gone to talk to his cronies about me.

I feel relieved, but anxious about the moment when he'll return too. I don't know whether he's going to continue to make comments like the one he's just made, or pretend that none of it ever happened.

Our meal finishes with the strong black coffee which makes my arms tremble like twigs in a storm for the rest of the evening.

I help wash the dishes and tidy the kitchen and then I wave some of my precious stash of paper and pencil at Kristina. She must understand that I want to go up to my tiny room and write my letters in privacy, because she waves me away with a smile.

I sit upstairs in the centre of the room and as there is no table, I write with my paper pressed against the wooden floorboards instead. I write two very different letters. The first is to Mama and Papa. I know that they will be worrying about me and I promised to write as soon as I was settled, even though we have no idea how long it will take the letter to get to Germany or even if it will get there at all.

Dear Mama and Papa,

Greetings from Chodecz. I've arrived safely and Kristina is being very kind to me. She has a son, Jakub, my brother, who is just over two years older than I am. The food here is very different, but I've been enjoying it anyway. The house is small and basic but very clean and I have my own room with a sloping roof and a single bed near the window. Anyway, you don't need to worry about me. I am in good hands. Hope you are both well.

Love,

Inge

I find it hard to sign off with my German name, but I know how they will feel if I don't.

When I've sealed this letter in an envelope and addressed it, I turn my attention to writing Wilf's letter. Writing to him brings him closer, as if he's sitting down by my side listening to me read the words straight into his ear. I imagine his face as he is reading it and I temper my letter accordingly, including things which will make him laugh and other things which will make him feel loved. Because he is Wilf, and we have no secrets, I also write this:

My so-called brother has called me "German pig". I do not know quite what I have done to deserve the title. But things are good with Kristina, Wilf. She is kind. When she took her headscarf off, I realized that she is very beautiful and not really old. She must have had me quite young. Anyway, I am starting to like her very much. I miss you, darling Wilf. I need one of your hugs. The ones where we block out the noise of the world and disappear into our own place for a while.
All my love,
Kasia

I seal this letter up too and put both near the door to remind me to ask tomorrow how I should post them. Then I go downstairs, praying that Jakub will not be there.

But of course he is, already sitting at the table slurping from a bowl of broth. He doesn't even look up when I come in.

Kristina flits between the sink and the table, putting more food in front of Jakub even though it is now almost midnight, and then taking the bowl away again to replace it with something else. Jakub lets out a slow belch at the end of the meal, for which he does not apologize although Kristina flaps a cloth at his head and shoots me a look of apology.

She goes outside into the backyard to check on the collection of red and black chickens who supply her with eggs every morning and I am left alone with my brother. My heart sinks. It seems rude for me to get up and leave, so I continue to sit with my cup of black coffee.

Jakub leans back in his chair and considers me. I do not like the expression on his face.

"So, German girl," he says. His German is slow but accurate. I guess he must have learned it at school. I know they learn German here and English too.

"What?" I say. I know it sounds rude, but so is he. "Why do you keep calling me German this and German that? I am a person, you know."

Jakub laughs. It is not a happy sound, but a harsh, dry bark.

"You are not a person," he says. "You are a German pig. Stolen by the Nazis and brought up by a Nazi father."

I'm so shocked that for a moment I can't think what

to say. Then I see a red mist rising up in front of my eyes.

"Okay," I say. "Yes. I was stolen by the Nazis. How do you think that makes me feel?"

Jakub shrugs. "I do not care how you feel," he says. "The Nazis murdered my father and broke the heart of my mother. So I do not care about Nazi-lovers like you."

I'm on the point of getting up and leaving the room, but then I think about what he just said.

"Another thing," I say. "My father is not, and never will be, a Nazi. He was a German soldier, and if you don't know the difference, you're more stupid than I thought. So wherever you get your false information from, you can stick it."

I sound strong, but underneath some sort of hole has opened up inside me. Much as I distrust Jakub, something about the certainty in his voice is troubling me. And it has made me distrust my parents again. I have believed their version of events because anything else would threaten to destroy my life completely. But now, if I stop to think about it, I can't remember how I know for sure that Papa was a German soldier, and not a Nazi. I'd always just assumed this to be the case because I know him to be a good man and Mama always told me he fought in the

German army. What if there are things about Papa that I'm not supposed to know?

What if they knew more about Lebensborn than they have let on?

This thought starts to haunt me. I push back my chair and leave the room, trying not to show him how much my arms and legs are shaking.

Then I go upstairs, fling myself face down onto the bed and sob for nearly an hour.

Chapter Thirty-one

OVER THE NEXT TWO WEEKS, Jakub continues to taunt me behind Kristina's back. He ignores me when she is in the room, but as soon as she leaves, he whispers "German pig!" to me and gives me his scornful smile.

I can't forget what he said about Papa either. I've been thinking hard about Mama and Papa and the way they've reacted ever since Kristina showed up at our front door. A cold chill of fear keeps creeping up inside me every time Jakub gives me his hard-eyed stare.

I try not to let it get to me. Kristina has introduced me to all her closest friends in the community and I spend part of each day in somebody else's house with her, watching the women chatter and cook and make beds and hang washing. After a while I am included in these arrangements and am allowed to peel vegetables and boil saucepans of water or hang undergarments across the fronts of the long, low houses until the wind blows them dry. Some of the women have children my age and I get to know and like some of the girls. There is a girl called Karin with a long, fair pigtail and a fresh complexion who I particularly like, who Kristina introduced me to during my first week in Chodecz. Sometimes I accompany her into the fields, where all the children who are on summer vacation from school are sent to help their parents with the farming. Although we don't speak much because of the language barrier, we smile and make faces at one another and I feel as if I am making a friend.

Because of Karin I gradually start to feel more welcomed and accepted in Chodecz. I keep reminding myself that I have a right to be here, because I was born here and this would have been my home had the woman in brown not snatched me away.

But Jakub does not accept me. And Kristina is unaware of the muttered hisses and taunts that he sends in my direction when she's not around. I feel as if I can't tell her because I am still the newcomer around here.

So I suffer it in silence, but the atmosphere between us is becoming tenser by the day. I wish that I could tell Karin at least, but I reckon she has a crush on my brother, because whenever he walks past us on the streets or joins us in the fields, her complexion becomes almost the same shade as the beets that we are picking and she turns away.

Towards the end of my third week I walk home from the fields, where I've spent a hot afternoon in the scorching sun, digging up vegetables and turning over the earth with a spade. I'm missing Wilf so much that it is now a permanent physical pain inside me.

I go up to my room to get changed out of my dress and I stop dead on the threshold.

The mirror on my wall is covered in red writing. I realize straight away that Jakub has gone through my belongings and found the one red lipstick that I brought with me from Mama's make-up bag, because my stuff is strewn all over the floor. Tears shoot straight up into my eyes and I feel sick. On the tiny mirror he has written this: *Your father is a Nazi. You are a Nazi-lover.*

I stand for a moment, trying not to feel dizzy. My own brother has rejected me. Ever since I arrived in Chodecz he has done nothing except look at me with scorn and hatred. My own flesh and blood. I think of Mama and Papa and tears rise up in my eyes again. Although they lied to me, they always treated me with love and kindness.

This is the thought that propels me into action.

I grab all my belongings from the cupboard and the

drawers and the floor and I stuff them any old how into my brown leather bag. I zip it up and lug it down the stairs with me into the kitchen. Kristina turns around and then stops when she sees the bag, and I just say, without taking a second to modify what comes out of my mouth, "I've had enough. I want to go home."

There is shock and hurt in Kristina's eyes. She sits me down at the table and makes me drink a hot cup of coffee, because she can see that I'm sick with emotion. Then she takes my hands in hers and just says, "Why?"

I can see her eyes are filling up with pain and anxiety, but I've got no fight left in me any longer. So I just say, "Your son is calling me a Nazi-lover, that's why."

Kristina understands enough of this to turn pale. Then she takes a deep breath. "You must ignore," she says. "Jakub's father, you know?"

She mimes a death slash to the throat.

"I know," I say. "I know that the Nazis stole your land and killed your husband. And I am sorry. But it was not my fault, and I am not a Nazi and neither is my papa."

A vision of Papa's kind face flashes up in front of me. I want to be with him so much that it hurts.

"I want to go home," I say, and as soon as I say it again, I know that this is indeed what I truly want to do.

Kristina looks down at the table for a moment. I see

that she is trying to compose herself. I feel wracked with guilt. We had just started to get to know one another, and she has been nothing but kind and loving to me ever since I got here. Now she risks losing me again, except this time I'm not being stolen off the streets by a woman in brown, but going home voluntarily of my own free will.

"I do not want you to go," she says in German, her voice low. "We have just come."

I feel tears rising up. I don't want to leave her, but I can't live with Jakub's bullying and I can see that it is only going to get worse.

"I need to go back to Germany," I say. "I'm really sorry."

Kristina moves closer to me.

"I ask you," she says. "Stay more days. Then go if you want. Yes?"

I look into the eyes of my mother and I remember how hard it has been for me to get here. It has been a journey in my head as well as a physical journey on a train. I feel agonized by this decision. I so want to go back to the normality of life with Mama and Papa. But I can see the pain in Kristina's eyes and something in me has remembered that I am not a girl who gives up easily on things.

"Okay," I hear myself say. "I will stay a little while longer."

Kristina's face softens with relief and she goes over to the sink to fill a pan with water.

I can hear Jakub walking around in the room next door.

"Right," I say to myself. "Don't let him get to you."

But deep inside my stomach, I feel sick.

Chapter Thirty-two

The next day is better.

But that's only because Jakub is working out in the fields from dawn until dusk and when he comes in, all he wants to do is eat and go to bed. We don't even look at each other now.

Kristina has obviously given Jakub a talking-to, because he is being short with her as well and she's got a helpless expression on her face every time he enters a room. She observes the horrible silence between us and I can see her thinking: how did a brother and sister end up with so little in common? Where is the love?

I try to get on with my days. I continue to learn some words of Polish with my mother and help her with the cooking.

But one day I go upstairs to my bedroom and find my clothes slashed through with a knife.

Everything except the dress that I am wearing is ruined.

I see red. I see great swirls of red mist. Those clothes were bought for me by Mama and they cost a lot of money. She chose them with care and love and now this boy has destroyed them.

I pound down the stairs, hoping that Kristina is not in and my prayers are answered. She is outside in the street, talking to a neighbour who is hanging sheets from a front window.

Jakub turns round when I enter the kitchen and for the first time I see a slight nervousness in his face. I think he can tell from the way I have burst into the room that I have finally lost my temper.

"What good will that do?" I say, standing by the small table with my hands on my hips. "What are you hoping to achieve by ruining all my clothes?"

Jakub turns back to the sink where he is scrubbing potatoes and he shrugs.

That shrug stokes the fire inside me and I find myself standing right up next to him.

"Have the guts to look at me," I say. "Or are you a coward? Hiding behind nasty words? That makes you just like the Nazis, doesn't it?"

Jakub flushes a deep red. "You're the Nazi," he says, although he still can't look me in the face. "You and your family. You should all be shot."

I can't believe I'm hearing this from my own brother.

I knock over a chair as I leave the kitchen, slamming the door behind me.

I ignore Jakub for the rest of that day. But, wherever I am, I feel his eyes cutting through me.

Nazi.

It is no good. I cannot stay here with my own brother hating me as much as he so obviously does.

I can't take it any more.

I need to go back to Munich.

Chapter Thirty-three

PAPA ARRANGED THAT OPEN RETURN for me and now I need to use it. So, three and a half weeks after I arrived in Chodecz, a tearful Kristina makes the necessary arrangements to get me onto the next train. Before long, a horse and cart pulls up outside the tiny house in Chodecz, as there is no bus for over an hour. I try not to remember the cart that took me away all those years ago as Kristina gets into it with me and we rattle away from the house where I was born.

This time I don't look back.

We don't speak on the journey to the station, but Kristina and I hold hands. I sense her sadness and my own begins to bubble up inside me until we are both trying to blink back tears without the other seeing.

I'm scared about making the long, lonely journey on my own. Even though Papa has written out every change of train and every name of every station very clearly, I remember that I struggled to make sense of it on the journey to Poland. With this I have the wallet of tickets and permits and passes that he so carefully compiled for me. Thinking of his kindness makes me indignant all over again at what Jakub has accused him of. I try to push the thought from my head, even though there was something about Jakub's expression that keeps replaying in front of my eyes. It was like he knew something that I didn't. But how can that be?

At the station, Kristina looks very small on the platform next to the large carriages of the train. She clasps both my hands in hers and looks into my eyes.

"You write," she says, miming a pencil and paper. "Yes?"

"Yes," I say. I kiss my mother's cheek and feel her release my hands, because the whistle has blown and I'm supposed to be on the train.

"Kasia," she says. "Kasia, Kasia."

I say nothing.

My heart feels as if it is going to split into two.

* * *

It is a long, long trip back. I lose track of the time at one point and when I wake from one of countless dozes against the window of one faceless train after another, I look out of the window with a panic and hope that I have not missed my station.

The border police do several more stringent checks of my identity papers and my heart is thumping so hard I'm sure that they must be able to hear it. They do not ask why a Polish girl is travelling to Munich, even though Papa warned me that they might and told me what to say – that I am visiting relatives on holiday. I realize that my innocent expression and long blonde plaits convince them that I am harmless and not worth causing a fuss over, so I smile and nod and thank them and sit with my knees together and my back straight.

I arrive back at the Marienplatz station at just after eight in the morning. I have been travelling for nearly twenty hours, as this journey took a longer route than my first one, and I am stiff and dazed and exhausted. I realize that as there has been no way of getting word to Mama and Papa about my unexpected return, nobody will be there to greet me, and I feel overcome with a sudden doubt about turning up on their doorstep unannounced.

I know where I will receive a warm welcome, however. So I shoulder my brown leather bag one final time, and set off on foot to the apartment that I love so well.

I trudge up the worn stairs of the building and knock on the green door with the blistering paint.

"Coming, coming," I hear Stefan say. He opens the door with his face half-shaved, wearing a white vest and a pair of pyjama bottoms, and stops with surprise and delight.

"Inge!" he says. "Or Kasia. What are you doing back?"

I realize that I am very tired at this moment. I begin to sway a little, and Stefan beckons me in with a concerned expression and sits me down in an armchair.

"You have come a long way, little one," he says, looking at my bag. "What happened?"

"I couldn't stay any longer," I whisper, looking around the familiar apartment with the photographs on the walls and the empty fireplace in front of me, the battered old black armchairs and the worn rug in the middle of the floor. "Oh, it feels so good to be back here."

He heads into the kitchen to make me a drink and something to eat. "Wilf will be back in a moment," he calls. "He's out on a job for me. Somebody locked themselves out of their office, the idiot."

I am passed a mug of hot chocolate and some bread and cheese. I consume both straight away.

"Could I stay here for a bit today?" I say. "I just need to get my head around going home again."

"Sure," says Stefan. "I have to go out to a job in a moment, but you can stay here until Wilf gets back. It will be a nice surprise for him. You must tell him what has happened to you. And he can tell me when I get back."

He leaves about five minutes later and I finish my food and drink and settle back in the armchair. It is so quiet and calm in here that I lean my head against the wing of the chair and drift off to sleep.

The next thing I feel is a gentle kiss on my forehead and a hand on my head.

I open my eyes and look straight into a pair that I love.

"Hello," Wilf says, in that soft, low voice which makes me feel special. "What are you doing in my chair?"

I don't speak. I fling my arms around his neck and bury my face in his shoulder. I cry silently, great heaving sobs of relief.

"Inge, you are strangling me," says Wilf, smiling at my tear-stained face. He pushes a strand of hair away from my cheek and gazes at me with those kind grey eyes which are so deep and full of love. I never want to stop looking into them.

"Sorry," I say. "I've just missed you so much."

"Why are you back so early?" he says after a while.

"I haven't had any of your letters yet."

I sniff and blow my nose on one of his blue handkerchiefs. "It turned out that my brother thought I was a Nazi-lover," I say. "He never let me forget it for one single moment. Kristina was brilliant but she couldn't stop him. So I had to come home."

Wilf's face has hardened. "He had no reason to say those things," he says. "You are a good person, and don't you forget that."

I lean back against him, feeling safe and warm and loved.

I stay with Wilf and Stefan for the rest of the day.

But by the time evening comes, I know I must go home to Mama and Papa. And I don't know how they are going to react. I don't want them to feel triumphant at my return, as if they were right all along to try to stop me going. I don't want them to think that I did not get on with Kristina. And I do not want to find that I get home and things are so different that I will never fit in there again.

"It's only been three and a half weeks," says Wilf, reading my mind as he so often does. He wipes my face with a clean handkerchief. "They love you. They will be so glad to see you.

"Come on," he says. "I'll take you back in the car."

* * *

We pull up outside the sleek modern house on the quiet close. Munich looks very grey and built-up after the vast sweep of cabbage and beet fields of Chodecz and the lake behind the church. I used to think that this house had a personality, but now I can't see it. The building just looks like a faceless square block.

Wilf leans over and kisses my cheek. "It will be fine," he says.

I inhale the smell of his jacket for a moment and close my eyes.

Then I get out of the car and head towards the house.

I ring the bell. I've got a key but I don't want to give anybody a fright.

It feels strange ringing the bell like a guest would. I remember when Kristina rang this bell for the first time and I realize what a lot of guts that must have taken and how nervous she must have felt, and I get a real pang of missing her. I realize that the quiet little woman in the headscarf started to take her place in my heart before I even left for Poland. Then I remember the mocking taunts of her son and the feeling fades a little. And while I'm thinking all this, the door is opened and Papa is calling out in surprise to Mama and I'm being enfolded in the biggest hug he's ever given me.

"What a wonderful surprise, pumpkin," he says, his moustache tickling my ear. "And I am so proud of you for making that journey on your own, even though I knew you would be fine."

Mama has come into the hall, white with shock. Her face, anxious and closed-off, breaks into a shy smile. "Inge," she says. She holds out her arms and, after a moment's hesitation, I walk right into them. She smells of fresh laundry and bread. I can see a new loaf sitting on the dining table behind her.

"What happened?" she says. "You were not supposed to come home yet."

I sigh. But it feels good to have Mama and Papa looking at me with such concern.

"Come and sit down," says Papa, pulling out a chair at the table for me and cutting some of Mama's bread. I bite into the soft white slice with a sigh of pleasure. I'm hungrier than I realized.

I tell them about Kristina's house and the little school and the smell of vegetables which is always in the air, and they smile and look interested and nod and ask questions.

"But why come back early?" Mama says.

I have already decided not to pass on the vile words

317

that Jakub spat at me. It is always difficult to bring up anything to do with the war in this house and I don't want to risk an argument when I have just got back to such a warm welcome. So I just say, "I did not get on very well with Jakub and the house was really too small for me to stay long."

Papa looks surprised. "I can't imagine anyone not taking to you, pumpkin," he says. "But then again, I'm your father, so I will always be on your side."

I smile at him. Despite everything, he still sounds and acts like a true father would.

"It is all fine now," I say. "I am back. That's what matters."

"Yes," says Mama with a warm smile. "That is indeed what matters."

But in the middle of the night, when I am back in my cosy bedroom with the white quilt and the soft pillows and the pink curtains and mellow lamplight, I sit bolt upright in bed and I hear Jakub's voice, loud, clear and nasty, in my ear.

Your father is a Nazi.

Chapter Thirty-four

IT IS THE TAIL END of the summer holidays. I have been back in Munich for just over a fortnight and I am dreading going back to school. I know that, just as I was teased in Poland for being German, I will be teased again in Germany for being born a Pole.

Still, I am happier than I have been for a long time.

Mama takes me shopping in town on Saturday as a treat and we sit in a cafe and eat chocolate torte together. She buys me some new clothes and a smart pair of shoes with little heels.

"You are old enough for a heel now, Inge," she says. "They do wonders for a woman's legs."

She stretches out her own legs and considers them for a moment. Like everything else about Mama, her stockings are impeccably clean and un-snagged and her shoes polished to perfection.

We have had such a nice afternoon that I feel closer to Mama and I decide to open up a little to her.

"Mama," I say. "You know that Kristina was good to me in Poland. But I did not tell you everything about her son. He kept saying that Papa was a Nazi. But we know that's not true, don't we?"

Mama's cup freezes halfway to her lips. Then she puts it down on the saucer with care.

"What a ridiculous thing to say," she says. "Your brother must be sick in the head. Papa was a good soldier. You know that."

I nod. "That's what I thought," I say.

But in my head I picture Jakub's face again. He didn't look sick in the head. He looked sly and certain and knowing.

I can't get what he said out of my mind. It buzzes at me like an annoying fly that just won't stop wanting to land on me. I swat it away. It comes back.

I have had this feeling before. When I went through Mama's drawers and found those letters from Kristina. It unsettles me. I have learned to trust my intuition when I get these feelings. I know that if I am having them, there's something, somewhere along the line, that needs looking into.

I keep remembering the ease with which Papa appeared to get all my papers together for the journey. Even Mr Schmidt could not do that, and he was something high up in the Foreign Office. So Papa must have had some good connections very high up somewhere.

And something about Mama's reaction to my question does not feel right. I keep remembering the way in which her cup froze halfway to her mouth.

I feel as if I can't let this go.

So I wait until Sunday afternoon, when Mama has gone out for a walk and Papa has gone to do extra paperwork in the office.

Then I put the chain over the front door just in case either of them come back early.

I start in Papa's study.

The drawer where I found the letters is still locked, but last time I looked, the only things in there were the letters themselves. So I leave that alone and turn my attention to Papa's desk instead. I sift through the pile of papers on top of it and find nothing of interest. Then I pull out every drawer in turn and rifle through various folders and books and stapled batches of papers. Most of it is just accounts and copies of invoices and bills, so I put it all back.

I try the bureau in the dining room but with no luck.

I go upstairs and try Mama's bedside cabinet again but there is nothing in there which I have not already seen.

I sit on the stairs for a while and try to think. I know that there must be other places in this house where things could be hidden. Then I look up at the loft hatch.

Of course.

I never go up there. I haven't been up there since I was a very little girl and Papa took me up and shone a torch into all the rafters and pretended that there were ghosts until I squealed to be taken downstairs again. My parents have always told me not to go up there because the boarding underfoot is unstable.

I open the hatch with a long-handled hook, pull down the ladder and inch my way up into the dark hole. Then I heave myself onto the boards of the loft and fumble for the light switch. A dim glow floods the attic and I can see various boxes stashed away in the corners. I crawl my way over, as the roof is very low, and I pull out a couple of boxes and start sifting through the contents. I find old dresses and rusty bits of kitchen equipment and then some garden tools and several old photograph albums with tiny black-and-white shots of people I don't recognize.

But my attention is caught by a painting which is leaning against the wall, half-obscured by a white sheet.

Part of the sheet has slipped and I can see the distinctive style of an artist I know well, because we've studied him at school. "Picasso!" I say out loud. I uncover the painting and stare at the angular lines of the face of his model. Yes. It's definitely Picasso. But what's it doing up here in the dusty attic and not displayed up on Mama's minimalist white walls downstairs? I put the painting down and pick up a couple of old boxes from the corner.

I sit in the middle of the floor and go through box after box and although some of the things are quite interesting, they're not giving me any clues. Then, just when I've realized that Mama will be back soon and I'd better be getting downstairs, I find a long dark-green box with a tiny gold key in the lock. Something about this box makes me pause before opening it. But the key is begging to be turned, so I do.

I open the hinged lid. Inside are two leather-bound diaries. Each has a date embossed in gold on the front. I pull out the first one, which is labelled *1944 Volume One*. I flick open the front cover. There's a page ruled with lines and margins and on the lines in a neat black scrawl is written: *Dachau journal. SS Krause.*

I reel back in shock. I look at the other volume. This is *1944 Volume Two* and again the name *SS Krause* is written in that same neat black handwriting.

My hand is shaking.

In my head I see the gates to the Lebensborn home in Steinhöring. Those forked black letters hammered into the iron pattern.

SS.

"No," I say to myself. "No. He can't be."

Papa.

I see those kind eyes and the soft brown moustache.

"Oh my God," I say to myself. "He has been lying to me. They have been lying to me. Again."

I turn the pages of one of the little diaries with my shaking hand. I don't want to read, but I know that I must.

There are many entries relating to the food eaten by prisoners, which seems to consist mainly of cabbage soup and bread. Notes that they must be given hot black coffee twice a day. There are other entries relating to visits to the camp by SS dignitaries. There are several entries relating to visits by Adolf Hitler, in a black scrawl with many exclamation marks.

My arm is shaking so hard now that I have to stop reading for a moment.

Dachau.

I know where that is. It is not far outside Munich. Wilf has told me about the women's camp which was set up there in 1944. It is where his mother spent the last year of her life, before she was sent to Riga by cattle truck and murdered there.

All the time, Papa has been lying to me.

When I have calmed myself a little, I pick up the diary and begin to read again. Some of what I am reading is mundane. Other things make me gasp. Words keep jumping out at me:

Action. Typhus. Gas. Killed. Liquidation. Epidemic. Suicide. Labour.

And one word seems to jump out more than any other. *Jew. Jew. Jew.*

Somehow I manage to get through the evening and behave normally with both my parents, even though I have a hard job looking Papa in the eye.

I need to speak to Wilf for comfort. But how can I? How can I tell him that my papa was a member of the SS at the camp whose name strikes fear and sickness into the hearts of Wilf and his father?

* * *

I do not sleep that night.

I know that before I challenge Papa, I need to do one last thing.

I need to visit Dachau.

Chapter Thirty-five

I CAN'T ASK WILF TO come with me. I just can't put him through that. But I know enough about Dachau to know that I should not go there on my own. In the end there is only one person I trust enough to ask.

She picks me up in her sleek blue car and we drive almost in silence through the outskirts of Munich and then a few kilometres outside.

Dachau is not open to the general public, but Marta's mother told me that if I wrote a letter requesting access, I would be able to arrange a visit. She said that I could use her address to receive the answer and avoid my parents intercepting the letter. So I did, with her help, explaining why I wanted to visit, and sure enough an official-looking letter arrived at the Schmidt house a few days later stating that I could come in the company of an adult and spend limited time at the site.

"They built these places away from the general population," says Marta's mother from behind her black sunglasses. She has been very kind and not asked many questions.

I did not tell Mama and Papa what I was doing, of course. I called out that I was going to see a friend and left before they could question me any further.

"Do you know much about Dachau?" I say.

"Not really," she says. "Only what I have heard on the radio, like everybody else in Munich. I know enough to be worried about the effect it will have on you today."

She sees my face and squeezes my hand. "It's alright," she says. "None of this is your fault. You are in shock. Come on. Let's get this over with."

And now Marta's mother is pulling up outside a vast grey space of low-lying buildings which stretch on as far as the eye can see. She kills the engine and a deathly hush falls over us. I have the window wound down, but I can't hear any birds at all.

She looks at me. I have used the drive here to tell her what I found in the loft.

"Are you sure about this, Kasia?" she says. "We don't have to go in."

I take in the sombre silence of this place. I feel dead in my soul already and we haven't even got out of the car yet.

"Yes," I say. "This is the final piece of my puzzle. I need to find out the truth about my parents once and for all."

We sign in at a small office on the edge of the camp. There's a subdued air even in here, and the man behind the desk does not smile, only looks at me for a second over the top of his glasses and then unlocks a door behind him and gestures us through.

We walk alongside railway tracks overgrown with grass and weeds. There is a stench coming up from them.

"Even now," says Marta's mother. "Even now you can smell death and disease here."

I find that I am holding her hand for strength.

We walk on, past low grey buildings which she tells me were barracks housing the camp prisoners. Marta's mother points out the women's barracks. It is so small that I can't believe it when she tells me that nearly a thousand women were crammed in here at any one time.

There is a wall around a courtyard with a smattering of black bullet holes visible in the brickwork. Neither of us says anything when we see that.

There is a building which was used as a crematorium

to burn the bodies of the diseased and starving prisoners. Inside there are vast metal ovens where the bodies were laid before burning. There's a palpable sense of evil in here and a stench of something sour and strong.

We leave this building and come to another which is partly underground and reached by a flight of stone steps.

We find ourselves standing in a long, low, unlit room. There are what look like shower heads positioned across the ceiling and a hatch in the middle. Marta's mother tells me that a deadly gas called Zyklon B was poured in to kill the innocent people who thought that they were being sent in to take a shower.

"Oh God," she says. Tears are running down her face. "How can human beings be so evil?" she says.

I say nothing. I am trying to convince myself, over and over, that my papa was nothing to do with this place. But his diaries say otherwise.

We come to a room with long lists of names printed on boards on the walls.

This is the room that was mentioned in the letter I received a few days ago. I have been dreading arriving at this place.

"Camp staff," says Marta's mother, glancing at me with unease. "Here you go, Kasia. If your father really did work here, his name will be on the list."

I start to run my finger down one of the lists and Marta's mother does the same with another. We work in silence, absorbed, grim, checking name after name. Suddenly I jump and trace my finger back to the name I've just passed.

"Here, here," I say to her, my voice cracking with despair. "Here. It says SS Krause. SS Krause. Look."

She comes over and follows my fingers.

"Oh, Kasia," she says, putting her arm around my shoulders. "I am so sorry."

At this point I become aware of somebody else looking at where my finger is pointing. I turn my head and find myself looking into a pair of watery blue eyes. They belong to a middle-aged woman with fair hair and a lined, tired-looking face.

"Excuse me," she says to me, never taking her eyes from my face. "Did you mention SS Krause?"

I nod. Through a voice thick with tears I ask, "Why?"

The woman laughs. It is a low, bitter sound. "How well I know that name," she says. "That name will haunt me until my dying day."

Marta's mother has stepped towards us and put a protective arm around me. "What do you mean?" she says. "Be aware that Kasia is still a child."

But the woman is staring deep into my eyes. "SS Krause destroyed my entire family," she says. "I am the only member left alive. And I only survived because I was here when the camp was liberated and I had just enough strength to crawl out of this hell."

My legs buckle underneath me. Marta's mother catches me just in time.

"You knew her?" says the woman to me. She still hasn't removed her eyes from mine. They bore right through me. "Krause? Are you family, or did you lose people in this place?"

"Family," I say in a whisper. "SS Krause. My father. That is his name on the board."

The woman gives that laugh again and shakes her head. "SS Krause was not a man," she says. "Although she had some things in common with them. Brute strength, for one."

I'm looking at the woman now, confused. For a moment I think that perhaps I have made some mistake and that there is another SS Krause.

"She had an unusually pretty name for one so evil," says the woman. "What was it? Oh yes. Anneli."

I fall. There's a fuss of voices and arms trying to lower me down and lift me up at the same time but I don't hear anything else after that.

SS Krause. The woman who assisted in the death of thousands and thousands of innocent people, including Wilf's mother.

SS Krause.

Mama.

Chapter Thirty-six

MY WORLD HAS COLLAPSED. I can't think straight. I can't think at all. The only image in my head is Mama now, but instead of seeing her in her usual shirt and blouse and shoes I now see my adoptive mother in the uniform of the SS with a swastika on the front and the eagle on her shoulder and she is not smiling any longer but stern, silent, forbidding, standing at the front of a queue of prisoners with their heads hanging low and she is shouting at them to get into line before dolloping thin grey soup into their metal bowls. I feel sick, sick to my stomach and I can't stop shivering.

I am put into Marta's mother's car and she drives me home, looking at me every few seconds with love and pain in her face.

"Do you want me to come in with you, Kasia?" she says. "You have had an enormous shock. And this is not going to be pretty. You may need support."

I shake my head. "No," I whisper. "But I have to ask you to pick somebody up. His name is Wilf and he's my boyfriend. He's a Jew. Mama and Papa don't know about him. I want him to come back with me. He needs to hear what I am going to say."

Marta's mother blows her cheeks out and gives me a look, but she takes a detour and follows my instructions. We pull up at Wilf's apartment. I go inside and knock on the door, my hand shaking and my legs unsteady. When Wilf opens the door he takes one look at my face and picks up his coat from the hook by the door, closing it behind him. He knows from my face that something serious has happened. I take him by the hand down the stairs of the apartment block and out into the street, then into the back seat of Mrs Schmidt's car. I sit in the back of the car with him while Marta's mother drives.

"Wilf, I have something terrible to tell you and it will give you a shock. I just want you to know that I had no idea of any of this until today," I say, shaking. "Wilf. My mother worked at Dachau as a member of the SS. I thought it was Papa, but it wasn't."

Wilf turns to me, colour draining from his face.

"What?" he says. "Surely that can't be right?"

I am crying openly now. Marta's mother is also crying and trying to subdue the sound.

"It is true," I say. "Wilf. I'm so, so sorry."

"Your mother…" says Wilf, his voice wavering. "Your mother was responsible for the death of mine."

"Oh, Wilf," I say through my tears. "I don't know what to say to you."

That is all I can say, and I say it several more times in the car. Wilf sits upright, pale and silent. He does not hold my hand and I do not force him to, even though I wish he would.

When we get to the close, Marta's mother kisses me on the cheek. "Come over any time," she says. "I am here for you."

I use my key and head straight in, Wilf behind me. I can hardly walk for trembling. It is not from nerves now though. It is rage.

I go into the dining room, the door banging against the wall behind me.

Papa comes out of the kitchen, sees my face and then Wilf and his smile fades.

"What is it?" he says. "What has happened? Who is this boy?"

I walk past him into the kitchen. Empty.

"Where is she?" I say. "Mama. Although I will never, ever refer to her as that again."

Papa stands looking lost as I pound through the house.

Mama is up in her bedroom, folding clothes into a pile and putting them in drawers.

I go over to her and take her by the arm.

"Inge," she says, laughing at first and then protesting as I grab her hard. "What are you doing? Stop that at once."

"Get downstairs," I say. "Get downstairs and come and face up to what you have done."

Mama stumbles as I pull her out of the room, but she comes without further protest. Her face has closed up and become impassive. I realize that she has often looked this way. Now I know what she was trying to hide behind her blank expression.

I drag her into the living room and stand her in front of the wall.

"Nobody else round here can afford a Picasso," I say. "But you have one in the loft under a blanket, Mother. Where did you get it from? Huh?"

Mama has gone very white. She sits down on the edge of a chair and glances at Papa. He shrugs his shoulders.

"She knows, Anneli," is all he says, but it's enough. And he has known too. All these years.

Wilf stands very quiet in the doorway, but Mama has noticed him.

"Who the hell are you?" she says.

I feel more anger building inside me. "He has a name," I say. "His name is Wilf and I love him. I have loved him for more than two years and I love him more than I could ever love you. And you are responsible for the greatest sadness and pain that ever happened in his life."

Wilf does not look at me. He is staring at Mama and she is now looking back at him with something dawning in her eyes.

"Don't tell me that he's a…" she says.

She can't say the word, so I say it for her.

"A Jew?" I say. "Yes. He is. You're not the only one who keeps secrets around here, Mother."

My voice is like that of a stranger. Bitter, clipped, harsh. It does not sound like a girl's voice, but that of an older woman.

Mama rises up from her chair and stares at me as if she does not know me.

"You bring a Jew into my house?" she says in a low voice. "You bring that filthy vermin into my house?"

Wilf stands his ground. "Some of us survived," he says. "You no longer have any power over us."

Mama makes as if to lunge towards him, but Papa holds her back just in time.

"Don't you have any conscience at all?" Wilf says. "For all those children who never got to grow up and have children of their own? For all the babies left without mothers, like me?"

Mama laughs. "We were just doing our job," she says. "Vermin like you needed to be got rid of, and that's what we did."

Papa has left the room. I hear him heaving great sobs in the kitchen.

"It wasn't Papa who arranged my identity papers, was it?" I say.

Everything is becoming clear now. Mama's obsession with order and control and cleanliness. The way she runs everything to a schedule. *The Nazis were afraid of disease and germs. The food was doled out to the Jews at the same time every morning.*

Her systems for everything, whether it's cooking or cleaning or tidying. *The Jews were systematically beaten and starved and murdered. The Nazis kept neat, detailed notes of every atrocity that was carried out in the camps.*

The way she never wastes food. The way she ladles out soup at home, as if she's thinking of something else. Her liking for strong, expensive black coffee and for making her own bread. *There was only dry bread and weak black coffee for the prisoners. If they were lucky, they received a ladleful of watery soup for their midday meal.*

How she disliked being enclosed. How she hated small rooms and lack of air. *The gas chambers were underground and the Jews were packed in like animals.*

Her money. *The SS helped themselves to valuables and money from the trainload of Jews who arrived in the camps every day.*

"You stole that Picasso from a Jew," I say. Everything is falling into place. "And that painting of Hitler. It's not Papa's, is it? It's yours."

I sit down, because my legs have given way.

Mama gives a brief nod. That's all. But now everything makes sense.

"Your father is not an innocent in all this," she says.

Papa comes in again at this point, blowing his nose.

"Papa?" I say. "What is Mama saying about you? Please tell me that you're not a Nazi too." Jakub's words ring through my head. *Your father is a Nazi.*

Papa comes over and takes my hands. I shake him off.

"I did work for the SS, yes," he says. "But I was not in the camps like Mama was. My first position was in offices at Ravensbrück where Mama was training to be an *Aufseherin* – an overseer. When she transferred to work at the new women's camp in Dachau, I came along to be near her, but again, I worked in an office role."

"Is that true?" I say to Mama. She gives a brief nod and, for once, I believe her.

But Papa still worked for the SS.

He is looking into my face.

"Inge," he says. "You'd better sit down. I've got something else to tell you."

I don't like the sound of this but I remain standing. Somehow, sitting seems to put me at a disadvantage.

"Your grandparents," says Papa. His face is grey. "They are still alive."

I start with surprise at this. I have always wished so hard to have grandparents.

"Where are they?" I say.

"Still in Munich," says Papa. "But they disowned Mama when they found out where she worked and what she did. You did see them once just after you came to us. But then they would not come any more."

I sink down into the leather chair behind me. This is too much to take in. "You have lied to me all my life," I whisper. "About where I came from. About how I got here. And now about what you did in the war. Why are you not in prison, Mama? Other Nazis were sent to prison. Why not you?"

Mama shrugs. Her face is like a blank canvas.

"They could not penalize everybody," she says. "There

were many of us. My Saturdays at Cafe Heck? I meet with others who worked at Dachau, just like me. They understand me. We understand one another and what we've been through. We need to support each other."

I can't believe I'm hearing this. *Every Saturday. Coming back pale and distant. I thought she was just tired.*

"What *you* went through?" I say. "What YOU went through? You should have gone to prison!"

Mama sighs. "I was not directly involved in the murder of prisoners," she says. "I worked in the finance department at the camp. It was hard for any court to prove anything against me."

I can hardly take a moment more of this.

"You're lying," I say. "I met a woman who remembered you. She talked about your brute strength. You belonged to an organization that stole from Jews. Beat Jews. Murdered Jews. You knew what was going on. You took part in it all. You are a Nazi-lover," I say. And Mama does not bother to deny what I am saying.

"Inge," says Papa, desperation in his voice, but I ignore him.

"My name is Kasia," I say, quieter now. "I will never use my German name again after today. And you will never be my parents again after today either."

Papa is sobbing, but Mama does not shed even a

single tear. She gets up, taking care not to look at Wilf.

"You don't understand," she says. "You will never understand. Life was dreadful in Germany before Hitler came. But if that is what you wish, then I will respect that. Despite everything I will always love you."

At that moment, I look into the face of the woman who has brought me up for twelve years and lied to me for all of them, and I see that her face shows nothing apart from being paler than usual. Nothing. There is no expression written upon her face and it chills me right through again.

"Things are what they are," says Mama. "I would do it all again if I had to. I dedicated my life to the *Führer*."

And with that, Mama walks out of the room and out of my life for ever.

I can see that Papa is in anguish. I sit down with him and with Wilf, who seems not to blame Papa even though he has admitted his work for the SS.

"How could you be married to somebody who was a killer?" Wilf asks.

Papa sighs. "I had no idea about the extent of her involvement when we first met in 1940, and we fell in love quickly. I met her at a dance near Ravensbrück where she was doing her training. By the time she was posted to Dachau in 1944 we were married and thinking about adopting you. We couldn't have our own children and the Nazis were offering children from Poland to those who could give them a good home. And then we took *you* home, Inge. We wanted you to have two parents. So even though what Mama did was not an easy thing for me to live with, I decided to stay in the marriage."

I hear what Papa is saying and I can also hear that he is contrite, but things have gone too far for me to go back.

I look at Wilf.

"Can you forgive me?" I whisper. This means more than anything. If Wilf can't forgive me, I might as well be dead.

Wilf comes over and crouches in front of me. He puts his hands on either side of my face and looks into my eyes.

"I love you," he says, "Kasia."

And that is all that he needs to say.

I ring the Red Cross again, thinking of those letters that began to arrive on my doormat soon after I was adopted. The letters that began all this. The letters which changed my life.

I tell the Red Cross my entire story. This time, because Papa has contacted them and given consent for me to be told whatever I want to know, they give me more information about the Lebensborn programme. It is just as the old man at Steinhöring told me. Children were sent from Poland by train to sorting centres in Germany, where they had their facial features assessed and measured to ensure that they fitted the Aryan ideal of Hitler's perfect German child. I was one of these children. Before I ended up in Steinhöring, I was housed at a temporary camp where Nazi officials decided that I looked fair enough to be offered up for adoption to German parents.

The children who did not measure up to the exacting standards of the Nazis were abandoned, beaten or sent to concentration camps where many of them died.

So I guess I was one of the lucky ones.

I move in with Wilf and Stefan straight away. I can't spend another night under the same roof as Mama. So I take over the little spare bedroom in Wilf's apartment and from that moment onwards, all the stress and worry begins to fall off me at last – although I know that it will take me a long time to recover from what I have discovered about myself and about Mama.

As Stefan is out a lot and Wilf often accompanies him on jobs after school, I have a lot of time to think about what has happened. I sit in the armchair where I curl up with Wilf and I reflect on the last few months.

I am happy living with Stefan and Wilf. We have always got along and now that I have my own little bedroom here I no longer have nightmares but sleep through the night undisturbed. At the weekends I have got a few hours' work serving behind the counter in the cake shop a few doors down from their apartment and I put this money towards helping to buy food for us all to eat.

It is a good existence and as time moves on I begin to distance myself more from my old life with Mama and Papa. I see Papa once a week and we go out to see a film or for a walk in the Old Town. But we never mention Mama, as I am still too angry inside to trust myself to speak about her. My loyalty is to Wilf and Stefan and it always will be. And Kristina. I now realize that my birth mother is everything I want and need a mother to be.

One day, I am walking over a bridge with Papa in late September and we are leaning looking down into the water. I keep sensing that he is about to say something important, so I don't interrupt with my own thoughts, and then he turns to me with tears in his eyes and says: "I am leaving her, Kasia."

Papa has been using my real name for a while now. Nobody refers to me as "Inge" any longer. Even my schoolmates have got used to calling me "Kasia", although it took some time for them to get used to it. Nobody calls me a "dirty Pole" any longer either.

I lean my cheek on Papa's shoulder.

"Where will you go?" I say. Neither of us needs to question what he has just said. Somewhere inside I feel a deep sigh of relief. I have always known that Papa's sense of what is right would break through in the end.

"I will stay in Munich," says Papa. "I want to continue at my job and I will need the money in order to rent an apartment. And of course I want to be near to you, pumpkin. That really is the main reason."

I smile into Papa's jacket.

"What about you, though?" he is saying. "What are your plans? Are you missing Kristina?"

I nod. I have been missing her a lot over the past two months. We have exchanged letters and photographs, but the post takes forever, so there are long periods of silence.

I want to go and see my mother again. My mother, my *Matka*.

The one who knows my name.

I also want to make my peace with Jakub. After all, although he did not behave well towards me, he was right in his suspicions about my parents. I am hoping that there is a chance we can reconcile and start again.

"I think," I say, "I think I would like to go back to Chodecz for a while. Could you help me with that, Papa?"

My father kisses the top of my head.

A week later, Papa turns up at Stefan's apartment and hands me an envelope.

"All here," he says, his eyes filling up with tears. "Will you drop me a line, Kasia? Just to say that you are okay?"

I nod.

I kiss him.

Then I start the preparations for my journey home.

Wilf and Stefan see me to the station.

I hold onto them as if I'm drowning and all three of us cry.

"I will see you soon," I say. But even though this is true, there is so much raw emotion in the air between us.

The train pulls out in a blaze of noise and steam. I do not look at them standing on the platform this time, because I know it will weaken me and I need to stay strong.

I wipe my tears and try to pull up that strength from somewhere deep inside.

I picture the grey-flecked eyes of Kristina and see her shy smile, her outstretched arms.

"I'm coming, Mama," I whisper.

I settle back into my seat. Then I watch the city disappear as I make my way back home.

My name is Hanna Michelson.

I am fifteen.
I am Latvian.

I live with my mother and grandmother.
My father is missing – taken by the Russians.

I have a boyfriend. When he holds my hand,
everything feels perfect.

I'm training to be a dancer.
But none of that matters now.

Because the Nazis have arrived, and I am a Jew. And as
far as they are concerned, this is all that matters.

This is my story.

USBORNE MODERN CLASSICS
introducing timeless stories to today's reader

Usborne Quicklinks

Many of the events and people mentioned in *The Stolen Ones* are based on historical fact. At the Usborne Quicklinks website you can find links to websites where you can discover what life was like in Nazi Germany and learn more about Hitler, Himmler, the SS, the Lebensborn program and Jewish persecution with newsreels, video clips, archive photographs and study guides.

To visit the links to the recommended websites for this book, go to the Usborne Quicklinks website at www.usborne.com/quicklinks and type in the keywords "The Stolen Ones". Please follow the online safety guidelines at the Usborne Quicklinks website.

The websites recommended at Usborne Quicklinks are regularly reviewed but Usborne Publishing is not responsible and does not accept liability for the availability or content of any website other than its own, or for any exposure to harmful, offensive or inaccurate material which may appear on the Web. Usborne Publishing will have no liability for any damage or loss caused by viruses that may be downloaded as a result of browsing the sites it recommends.